BUYER BEWARE

Can you tell the difference . . .

+ Between solid gold, gold-filled, and gold-plated?

+ Between 14K and 24K gold?

+ Between sterling silver, Britannia standard, German silver, and Sheffield plate?

+ Between a natural pearl, a cultured pearl, and a mother-of-pearl?

+ Between platinum, palladium, and rhodium?

+ Between a brilliant, emerald, or marquise cut?

+ Between glass, paste, and a real gemstone?

+ Between a genuine antique and a fake?

Whether you're buying a diamond engagement ring, Native American pieces, or antique jewelry, Anne Bingham's guide tells you everything you need to know to get the most for your money and buy jewelry you can treasure forever.

BUYING JEWELRY

Everything You Need to Know Before You Buy

ANNE BINGHAM

HarperPaperbacks
A Division of HarperCollinsPublishers

Harper Paperbacks   *A Division of* HarperCollins*Publishers*
10 East 53rd Street, New York, N.Y.
10022

A paperback edition of this book was published in 1989 by McGraw-Hill Publishing Company.

Cover photographs of Hand With Pearls courtesy of The Stock Market/Morris Lane, of Gold & Diamond Rings courtesy of The Stock Market/Karen Leeds, of Gold Chains courtesy of The Stock Market/Michael Furman

First HarperPaperbacks printing: March 1994

Printed in the United States of America

Harper Paperbacks and colophon are trademarks of HarperCollins*Publishers*

10 9 8 7 6 5 4 3 2 1

For Jim,
the most precious gem of all

Contents

CONTENTS

1

It's a Jungle Out There

Buying jewelry is a risky business for the uninitiated. Without a working knowledge of the vocabulary you can easily end up with something
of inferior value, for which you have not necessarily paid an inferior price. True, there are only
a few metals in the precious category, but gemstones are another matter. Some two dozen
chemical elements are involved, combining in at
least a hundred different ways to produce as
many different effects. Quartz, for example,

comes in transparent, translucent, and opaque versions, in every color, with most varieties having more than one name in common usage.

Furthermore, there are no "bargains" in fine jewelry. Although you and your checking account might be taken for a ride at a "borax" operation, in any reputable store you get just what you pay for. If you are unaware of the difference in quality between gems, you might settle for a stone of less quality than what you actually want. It's one thing to make a *deliberate* compromise in quality. It's quite another to discover, years later, that the engagement ring you selected with the naive understanding that "diamonds are always a good investment" wasn't such a good investment after all.

There are diamonds, and then there are diamonds. Only a small percent are sufficiently free from flaws, and cut with the required skill, to qualify as precious gems. But the others—the miscuts, the flawed, the off-colored—are still on the market. You've seen them advertised:

Genuine one-carat DIAMONDS at the UNBELIEVABLY LOW PRICE OF $39.95!

They might be diamonds according to chemical analysis, but gem-quality stones they ain't, my friend. The same goes for rubies, emeralds, amethysts, pearls, cat's eyes, and coral. The key phrase here is "gem quality." Inferior versions of every gem-quality stone are on the market, and although they may very well be chemically genuine, you'd be better off putting your money into a good, gem-quality synthetic.

Keep in mind, too, that an adjective used with a gemstone's name may qualify more than the color of the stone. Smoky topaz, for example, often isn't topaz at all, but a variety of quartz. Good topaz quartz is a fine gemstone, but it's *not* topaz.

Similarly:

- Mexican onyx is not true onyx.

- A Brazilian emerald is not the same as an emerald from Brazil.

- Simulated pearls never saw an oyster.

- All green stone carved with Oriental figures is not jade (nor, for that matter, is all gem-quality jade colored green).

- A three-carat diamond and a three-carat sapphire are neither of equal size nor equal value—and if you can touch either for less than a down payment on a good three-bedroom home close to school and church, it's probably not worth your time.

A jeweler of integrity will tell you these things. A clerk from the watch department, subbing behind the ring counter while the regular clerk takes a phone call, may not know enough about the merchandise to be able to give you good guidance, no matter how sterling his or her motives. Throwing yourself on the reputation of the store may not do you any good in a suburban mall store that caters to the marriage and grandmother trade; the "best in the house" may not be as good as you could find elsewhere. There's just no substitute for being an informed consumer. This doesn't mean that you will need a high degree of technical knowledge. All that's really necessary is the ability to ask the right questions.

Having managed to escape the merchandising perils, you'll also need to know how to take care of your expensive jewelry once you've purchased it. Advertising to the contrary, a diamond is not "forever" if badly treated. True, it's one of the hardest substances on earth, but hardness and toughness are not quite the same thing. The classic "see if it scratches glass" test will put a streak on the mayonnaise jar, all right, but it also can cause the diamond irreparable harm.

The harder gems can survive benign neglect because dirt, face powder, or cat hair caught in the mounting can be remedied with a good sudsing. However, treat pearls to a bath and you might as well run them through a food processor. Never mind that they grew up in the water; once they leave the oyster their needs undergo a dramatic change.

Where and how you wear the more fragile gemstones is important as well, and we're not talking social graces here, we're talking survival. Opal earstuds are not appropriate for cross-country skiing; the temperature can destroy them even if you survive unscathed.

Beyond physical care, it's important to have fine jewelry insured. Stones can drop from their settings; necklaces can break; one of your offspring can decide to play buried treasure with your brooches. Then there's the unpleasant possibility of being asked to relinquish your jewelry involuntarily in a parking lot, or of having someone drop by while you're away from home to save your heirs the bother of quarrelling over the disposition of your parure.

This book won't prepare you to speculate in gems and precious metals. For that, you'll need much additional knowledge, vast sums of money (preferably old, so you'll have the family's reputation to borrow against when you take a bath in the market), a daredevil disposition, and reasonable clairvoyance. It's a fair assumption that if you have any two of these qualities, you wouldn't be reading this book in the first place.

Nor will the information in the chapters that follow make you an expert. Acquiring an appraiser's expertise or a jeweler's eye requires specialized training. But while you may not be able to distinguish between treated and untreated turquoise at a glance, you will learn enough not to fall for a squash blossom necklace on sale at the state fair. You will be able to determine once and for all if your grandmother's necklace is glass or rock crystal. You probably will be able to spy a fake pearl, although you won't be able to detect the naturals from the cultured without special equipment. And you will learn what to ask and what to look for, whether you're making your purchase in a retail store or from a custom goldsmith.

Two final cautions:

1. Don't become a jewelry snob. Costume pieces have their place. The "pearls" your daughter buys you with her paper route money are as precious as—or more so than—the finest strand from the Persian Gulf. Turning away from a lovely shell cameo because it isn't onyx misses the point, which is the not inconsiderable skill it takes to carve in bas-relief on anything.

2. Be discreet with your knowledge. Don't destroy other people's illusions about their treasures. To observe to anyone other than your spouse that the guest of honor's earrings show entirely too much fire to be anything other than cubic zirconia is merely catty. To point out that your employer's watchband is stabilized turquoise . . . well, if you're that foolish, you probably don't deserve a promotion anyway.

2

$\blacklozenge$

All That Glitters Isn't 14K

If you've watched more than three movies made during the heyday of the Western, you know that grizzled old prospectors died of broken hearts by the thousands upon discovering that their hard-won claims were nothing but iron pyrite. "Fools' gold," says the sheriff, shaking his head as he examines the nuggets in the poor geezer's poke.

Old-time movie sheriffs were good at such eyeball assays; perhaps they took correspondence courses during the winter when rustlers and gunslingers were snowed in. They were the first and last of their kind, though. Gold doesn't yield its secrets that easily.

WHY GO FOR THE GOLD?

Although iron pyrite and any number of copper alloys can duplicate a credible gold color, and other metals are more rare, gold has qualities that make it a metal without peer in a world that prizes ornamentation. Gold doesn't tarnish, rust, corrode, or fade in color. It survives smog, salt, water, and 10,000 years in the tomb of an ancient queen. It's so permanent, in fact, that it took alchemists centuries to figure out how to dissolve it; and when they finally hit upon the right combination of acids (nitric and hydrochloric), they named the solution *aqua regia* ("royal water") because it could dissolve the most royal of metals.

Further, gold is ideally suited to ornamentation. It can take almost any shape, a property called *malleability*. It can be hammered into a sheet so thin it's practically transparent, and drawn into a wire so fine it can barely be seen—a virtue called *ductility*. It's said that one troy ounce of gold can be drawn into a wire 50 miles long, although why anyone would want to do so is unclear.

As a result, gold can be shaped into almost any form of ornamentation that designers can come up with (witness the cunning little bees, tennis rackets, and other minutiae that show up in Tiffany's Christmas ads). All this flexibility has a drawback, however. No matter how strong gold may be on the international metals market, gold is a relative weakling when it stands alone. On the scale of hardness used to measure the strength of minerals (see Chapter 5), pure gold sinks near the bottom. The previously mentioned 50-mile gold wire would snap at the brush of a feather; a ring of pure gold would easily bend out of shape.

GOLD ALLOYS

As a result of its relative softness, gold usually is mixed with one or more additional metals to strengthen it. Copper and silver are the usual metals; occasionally nickel or platinum also are used. When another metal is mixed with gold, the result is an *alloy*.

The metals used in an alloy not only strengthen the metal but also determine its color. *Yellow gold,* which usually contains equal amounts of copper and silver, is the alloy most people know as gold. An alloy of gold, copper, and nickel or platinum, with a trace of zinc, results in *white gold*. Nickel makes the alloy very white and somewhat brittle, while copper brings the color back toward silver and restores a bit of flexibility.

Pink gold, sometimes called *rose gold,* has more copper than silver in the alloy, and *red gold* has even more. Pink and red golds frequently are found in jewelry that originates in the Orient. *Green gold* has silver as the main component of its alloy, along with zinc and copper in the lower karatages. If you have any of the tourist jewelry sold in the western United States as "Black Hills gold," what you probably have is a piece with pink and green gold motifs on a yellow gold background. A *purple gold* alloy, made with aluminum, resembles an opaque amethyst.

WHAT "KARAT" MEANS

Gold and the other precious metals are measured in ounces, but not in the avoirdupois system of 16 ounces to a pound that's familiar to United States citizens (see Table 1 in the Appendix). Gold is measured instead on the ancient troy standard, also known as apothecary weight, used by pharmacists and the medical profession. A *troy ounce* is equivalent to 1.097 avoirdupois ounces.

11

The purity, or fineness, of gold is measured by the *karat* (in most English-speaking nations the word is spelled "carat" when referring to metal fineness as well as gemstone weight, but in the United States the "c" spelling is reserved for measuring gemstone weight). The word probably dates to ancient times when the seeds of the carob plant were used as a measure of the weight of gemstones, one carob seed approximating 200 milligrams, roughly equivalent to today's 200 milligram gemstone carat (see Chapter 5). Carob, more familiar today as a low-fat substitute for chocolate, has a seed pod containing 24 horn-shaped seeds of uniform size and mass (the Greek word for carob seed means "little horn"). It's thought that the term also became extended to the fineness of gold after the Roman conquest of Greece—with pure gold afforded the designation of 24 karat.

The purity of gold is measured on a scale of 1 to 24, with 24 karats (abbreviated as 24K) being the purest form of the metal. Standard alloys in use in the United States are 18K (meaning 18 parts out of 24 are pure gold—in other words, the alloy is 75% pure gold, 25% other metal), 14K (14/24ths, or 58.3% pure), 12K (12/24ths, or 50% pure), and 10K (10/24ths, or 41.6% pure).

Alloys vary from country to country and from era to era. Many antique wedding rings are a soft 22K alloy, which explains why a well-worn ring will have thinned almost to the breaking point over the years, while a modern, more durable 22K alloy is the standard for many European wedding rings today. Imported gold pieces often have the karat weight expressed in fractions or decimals rather than the K format. Thus, $750/1000$ and .750 both are equivalent to 18K, and $585/1000$ and .585 are equivalent to 14K. And just to keep things interesting for the traveler, the number of recognized standards varies from country to country. Japan, for instance, recognizes nine grades of gold between $1000/1000$ (24K) and $375/1000$ (9K), while Italy recognizes only five, the lowest being $333/1000$ or .333 (the equivalent of 8K), and the highest alloy being $750/1000$ (18K).

Federal Trade Commission rules require that all jewelry material sold as gold in this country be described by "a correct designation of the karat fineness of the alloy." A piece cannot be sold simply as "gold" without further qualification unless it's made from pure, unalloyed 24K gold; there are some pieces like that around, manufactured primarily for sale to investors. As jewelry, they're poor risks; they simply won't hold up well under normal wear.

While the word "gold" can't stand alone in an advertisement or marked on a piece of jewelry, the karat markings can. In fact, a piece seldom is stamped "14K gold"—"14K" is the more usual marking. Federal Trade Commission rules also require commercially produced contemporary pieces sold in this country to carry the manufacturer's trademark if karatage is specified on the item, but vintage and antique pieces, or items purchased abroad, often will have only a karat marking.

GOLD COATINGS

A piece of less than solid 14K is usually considered *costume jewelry;* anything less than 10K definitely is, and may not be sold in the United States as gold jewelry. The same applies to any piece of a less precious metal coated with gold. There are a number of ways to coat a baser metal with gold.

Vermeil means gold-coated silver if the piece is very old or very contemporary. If it's vintage or antique jewelry, or something purchased abroad, vermeil can mean gold-coated bronze, brass, copper, stainless steel, or whatever was cost-effective for the manufacturer. The FTC standard for contemporary vermeil jewelry requires the underlying metal to be sterling silver (see Chapter 3), coated with a minimum of 120 millionths of an inch of gold.

Plated and gold-filled jewelry results from

bonding sheets of gold or gold alloy to a base metal through heat, a chemical process, or pressure. *Gold-filled* applies if the gold coating is 1/20th or more of the total weight of the piece. (See Figure 1.) Gold-filled pieces must be marked with the fractional weight of the gold alloy, such as "1/20 14K GF" (which means that 1/20th of the total weight of the piece is 14K gold). Abbreviations are the norm; there isn't room to be chatty on the back of an earring or on the nib of an expensive fountain pen.

When the surface layer of gold is less than 1/20th of the weight, the terms *gold-plated, gold overlay,* or *rolled gold plate* apply. All commercial gold plating in this country today is done through a chemical electroplating process that bonds the gold to the base metal. Gold plating with a minimum thickness of 100 millionths of an inch is called *heavy gold electroplate.* This is more desirable than plain *gold electroplate,* which has a minimum standard of only 7 millionths of an inch. *Gold-flashed* or *gold-washed* designates anything thinner than gold electroplate.

Costume pieces labeled *goldtone* or *golden metal* have a superficial resemblance to gold, but they have no actual gold in their composition.

Gold

Metal

Solid Gold   Gold-filled   Gold-plated

FIGURE 1.   Cross sections of solid gold, gold-filled, and gold-plated metal (not drawn to scale).

GOLDEN TRIVIA

Bullion (pronounced *bull*-yon) is pure, unalloyed gold formed into bars, ingots, or plates. Bullion is sold by the troy ounce, generally in multiples of 100 to 1,000 ounces, and by the kilogram. This is the stuff that's sold on the international markets and stored at Fort Knox and in bank vaults around the country.

Bouillon, on the other hand, is sold by the avoirdupois ounce because it's soup, not metal. It's pronounced something like *boo*-yawn; only native speakers of French can get it completely right. It's important for you to practice both spellings and pronunciations, lest you be discovered holding forth on the price of chicken soup on the London exchange.

Because of gold's resistance to corrosion, the value most cultures have given it, and the ease with which it can be recycled, it's sometimes said that most of the gold ever mined is still in existence. It's true that jewelry has been melted and remelted over the centuries to make jewelry that fit the prevailing fashion or prevailing currency. Some gold is squirreled away in national treasuries and bank vaults in the form of bars and ingots, coins and medallions. Some of it is back underground, buried with the ancients in yet-to-be-discovered crypts. Lots of it is supposed to lie at the bottom of the sea lanes between the New World and Spain.

But that's not quite the whole story. Some years ago atomic scientists achieved what untold generations of alchemists were not able to do—turn base metal (lead) into gold, which added a quantity (admittedly, a minute quantity!) to the world's gold supply.

And because some gold surely was converted into energy in the destruction of Hiroshima and Nagasaki, claiming the constancy of the world's supply probably would be challenged in a gathering of sensitive activists. But then again, you might be able to get away with it; activists have more to worry about than the absolute quantity of gold available in the world.

3

Silver and
Other Precious Metals

Gold isn't the only game in town. In the last century, there was a time when aluminum, newly discovered and difficult to refine, was considered a precious metal. Today, depending on who designs them, certain steel pieces command a fair price. Generally speaking, however, silver and the platinums are the main alternatives to gold.

SILVER AND ITS ALLOYS

Silver has many of gold's good qualities, including a pleasing color (usually described as "brilliant white") and great malleability. It can be drawn, cast, forged, and shaped with the same techniques used for gold, and it also can be pounded so thin (to about 1/100,000th inch) that light will shine through.

It also shares some of gold's drawbacks. Like gold, pure silver is too soft to be fashioned into anything that will be subjected to even mild wear. It's usually alloyed with copper to increase its strength. The most familiar silver alloy is *sterling,* a term in use since medieval times. Sterling is an alloy of 925 parts pure silver and 75 parts copper. Although karat terminology is never applied to silver, sterling is the equivalent of 22K fineness in gold.

A somewhat purer alloy at 958 parts pure is the *Britannia standard,* today usually found only on genuine or reproduction pieces from the Queen Anne era. The Britannia standard was imposed for jewelry and utensils in Great Britain from 1697 through 1719 in order to discourage smiths from melting down coins, which had a lower silver content.

Establishing the Britannia standard was necessary in order to discourage production of *coin silver* articles, manufactured by melting down silver money. It has been some time since a nation has minted sterling coin except for ceremonial or numismatic purposes. The fineness of most old coin silver varies with the quality of the original coins, but generally is around the .900 mark. American Indian jewelry formerly was made to this fineness, but those who know their squash blossom necklaces say the best Native American designers now use sterling. Old Indian jewelry, fashioned before the turn of the century when laws against melting coins weren't enforced, was made from either United States coins or Mexican pesos; pieces made with the latter have a blue cast because the peso alloy contained less copper than the United States alloy.

Pawn silver describes not the composition of the metal but its use. Again applying to American Indian jewelry, it refers to the custom of Southwest tribal members to turn their family's silver over to a pawnbroker during hard times, and just as regularly redeem it when the crops came in—the frontier equivalent of getting a farm loan from the bank. Pawn silver properly applies only to jewelry made before World War II; after the war, the system fell into disuse. An authentic pawn silver piece has no greater intrinsic value than an identical non-pawn piece, although sometimes documented history will add to the price of a piece.

The metal known as *German silver* isn't silver at all, but an alloy of copper (65%), zinc (17%), and nickel. Also known as *nickel silver,* it's used for imitation silver pieces as well as a base for silver plating.

White metal is another silver look-alike. It's an alloy of 90% tin, 9% antimony, and a smidgen of copper.

Unlike gold with its numerous karat designations, silver terminology remains fairly simple. Either it's sterling, or it's not. If a metal is silver-plated, the plating is pure silver rather than an alloy; Federal Trade Commission rules prohibit the use of "sterling" or "coin silver" in reference to a plated article.

Sheffield plate refers to a method of fusing a silver coating onto a copper core. The first silver-plating process to be a commercial success, it is named for its birthplace, the foundry town of Sheffield, England. Today, silver plating is generally done by electroplating. The thickness of the silver layer determines the durability of the coated object; a silver-plated bracelet needs a thicker coating than a pair of silver-plated earrings. Unlike gold plating, however, there are no standards for marking a silver-plated piece to denote the thickness of the silver.

SILVER'S DRAWBACKS

Silver might be considered as valuable as gold were it less abundant and less eager to combine with airborne sulphur. This latter factor is silver's only real flaw—it tarnishes. Tarnish actually is a protective coat, beginning as an almost imperceptible jaundice and deepening to brown and, finally, to smudgy black. The process is quicker in the polluted air of today's cities, less rapid in the open countryside unless you're downwind of a coal-burning factory. Silver also is sensitive to some alkali compounds, so exposure to sea air doesn't do it much good, either. When rounding the Horn, leave your sterling behind.

Tarnish can be slowed if traces of arsenic and antimony are added to the alloy. Rhodium plating avoids the problem altogether, but at a cost to the mellow patina that adds so much to the aesthetic value of old silver.

Much of the silver mined today comes from Mexico. Other significant suppliers are Canada, the United States, Peru, and Russia. Not all of it ends up in jewelry or coins; nearly a third of the annual output of silver is consumed by the graphic arts industry.

PLATINUM

In contrast to gold, which has been fashioned into jewelry for eons, platinum didn't become jeweler's material until the early 1900s. It wasn't even discovered until 1557, 1735, or 1750, depending on which source you read.

"Platinum" refers both to a specific metal and to a group of six related metals, most of which have names suggesting they'd be at home in the defense industry: platinum itself, palladium, rhodium, ruthenium, iridium, and osmium. They're all jumbled together in their natural state, and a complicated chemical process is necessary to separate them.

Platinum, the most familiar of the group, is nearly as easy to work as silver, which it resembles in color. The name itself, in fact, derives from a Spanish word for "silver." It doesn't tarnish, though, and it's quite strong when alloyed, usually with other metals in the platinum group, making it especially useful for delicate "hidden" settings of precious stones.

Palladium is pearly gray in color, and is sometimes used instead of nickel or silver in the finest white gold. More plentiful than platinum, it's correspondingly less expensive, and because it's lighter in weight, it's especially suited for inlay work. Palladium is sometimes alloyed with ruthenium or rhodium for hardness.

23

Rhodium is a silvery, highly reflective metal, usually used in the jewelry industry for electroplating base metal objects. Although sometimes silver is electroplated with rhodium to prevent tarnishing, it's important to remember that all rhodium-plated silver is not necessarily sterling—although it's a fraudulent practice, silver plate can be coated with rhodium as well.

Iridium, ruthenium, and *osmium* are the three most dense substances known to science. Osmium is twice as heavy as lead; the others are not much lighter. Since a little goes a long way, these metals are used by jewelers mainly in alloys to strengthen platinum, palladium, or one another. Most other applications are industrial; occasionally one will show up on the nib of a fountain pen.

The platinums are abbreviated as Pt., Pd., Rh., Ir., Ru., and Os. When "platinum" appears alone on a piece, the fineness of the total platinum group is .985, with at least .950 being pure platinum and no more than 50 parts being other metals (or, if the item is soldered, .900 platinum and .950 platinum plus related metals). When the name is preceded by the name of a related metal, such as "iridium platinum" or "ruthenium platinum," the platinum content is .750, the related metals are .200, and the remainder is solder. When the platinum content is less than .500, the metal may not be marked platinum at all, but may be marked palladium, iridium, or ruthenium, provided the total platinum and related metals content is .950, soldered or not (for example, 450 Pt., 500 Pd.).

4

Metal Alone

While a gemstone is rarely worn entirely by it-self unless it's gracing the navel of an exotic dancer, precious metal is often a stunning deco-ration all by itself, especially if enhanced by skillful design.

The quality of the finished piece depends in large part on the techniques used to transform the metal from an ingot, sheet, or coil of wire in a factory or metalworker's studio.

HOW METAL IS SHAPED

Simple pounding and twisting will shape metal to some degree, and heat softens it and makes it easier to work. *Cast* pieces are formed by pouring melted metal into a mold. If the piece is to be one of a kind, the mold is deliberately destroyed after the casting has hardened. If mass production is the goal, the mold is used again and again. *Lost wax* is a casting process in which a wax model of the finished piece is encased in a sand or plaster mold. The mold is then heated and the wax drained out (or "lost"), and hot metal is poured through a small opening into the impression left by the wax model. When the metal cools, it hardens into the shape of the wax model.

Forging, in the metalwork sense, means shaping the metal by heating it and pounding it into shape. Forging may be done manually village smithy style or by machine. Handmade forged pieces usually are stronger than cast pieces because the pounding forces the grains of metal closer together to form a tighter bond, although commercially produced cast pieces are comparable in strength to commercially forged pieces.

Although chains can be made from forged links, they frequently start out as a coil of wire. So do earring loops, pins on the back of brooches, and *filigree* (delicate openwork made with fine gold or silver wire curled, twisted, or braided together). Wire comes in a variety of diameters, called *gauges,* as well as numerous textures and strengths. All wire is drawn, which is a process that progressively reduces the diameter of the wire by pulling (drawing) it through a series of dies in a machine or holes in a *drawplate,* a metal plate punched with holes corresponding to standard wire gauges. Hand-drawn wire is found today only on handmade pieces. Drawing can be repeated as often as necessary to achieve the desired diameter.

HOW METAL IS DECORATED

Forming the metal is only the first step. How it's finished and decorated plays a major role in its beauty. Polishing is one of the simpler finishes. If a piece is *bright polished,* it has a high, reflective shine. If it's *plain polished,* it has a soft glow. *Patina,* a soft glow that develops from years of wear and exposure to air, can be simulated by dulling the surface with a fine abrasive such as pumice and a metal brush known as a scratch brush. A scratch brush also creates a flat, non-reflective surface called a *brush finish* or a *matte finish* (sometimes spelled "mat" or "matt"). A matte finish with a soft, pearly luster is a *satin finish.*

A *frosted finish,* also called a *sandblast finish,* is produced by blasting the surface with a highly pressurized stream of sand, on the same principle as the process used to clean facades of stone buildings.

Chemical Treatment

Chemicals can produce different textures as well. A design can be *etched* onto the surface by dipping the piece in acid, which eats into the metal except where it has a protective coating. *Black finishing,* or *oxidizing,* works the same way, using a chemical that "burns" the surface of the metal and causes it to turn black. The oxide usually serves as a background for a polished, raised design, but it also can be the field for engraving.

Other chemical treatments that provide a contrast to a polished or engraved design are *rose finishing,* which puts a pink smudge on yellow gold, and *Indian finishing,* which puts an olive smudge on green gold.

Tooling

If the metal is cut away or pushed to one side, the piece is said to be *engraved.* Small chisels are used for this process. When the cut has beveled edges that sparkle, the piece is said to be *bright cut. Niello* (pronounced nee-*ell*-o) is an engraved design that has been filled with a blue-black alloy. *Piercing* penetrates portions of the metal so that a cutout design results.

Chasing is a technique that refines designs without removing any metal. Small blunt tools are hammered around or against a design to raise it up from the surface, to push it down into small valleys, or to push it to one side.

Metal can also be decorated without chisels. An *embossed* design is hammered or stamped onto the piece from the front. *Repoussé* (pronounced ree-poo-*say*) is worked from the back. *Swedging* is an embossing technique that forces the metal into the grooves of an iron block. The resulting piece is grooved both front and back and frequently shows up on pieces worked in the Native American tradition.

Decorating Metal with Metal

Sometimes metal is decorated with other metal. *Appliqué* involves soldering a separately crafted design onto another piece of metal. *Inlay,* or *damascene,* means that one metal is set into the surface of another, and usually ground flush with the surface of the larger piece. (Damascene also sometimes refers to a moiré-like pattern on the metal.) *Overlay* means that a cutout design is made in one piece, which is then soldered to a second piece. *Gadrooning* is the

30

attachment of stamped or cast convex curves which are set vertically or slightly spiralled in a row. *Granulation* is a dense covering of very tiny metal balls.

The various methods of gilding and electroplating are described in the chapters on gold and silver, but it's appropriate here to discuss some special finishes given to plating. An *English finish* is a highly polished surface of 24K gold electroplate; a *Roman finish* is 24K electroplate softened to a glow by a scratch brush. An *acid finish,* also known as depletion gilding, is a way of enriching the surface of the precious metal by making it more closely resemble the color of pure metal. It's accomplished by dipping the finished piece into an acid that removes some of the alloyed metals from the surface.

Enamel

Enamel is powdered glass that has melted and fused to the underlying metal after being baked in a kiln. It's an ancient form of decoration brought to a high art in many cultures, including that of medieval Europe, which probably explains why a knowledge of French is helpful in pronouncing the techniques.

When the enamel is in the spaces between metal strips or wires soldered onto the surface of a backing metal, it is called *cloisonné* (claws-

zun-ay), which is especially prevalent today in good costume jewelry from the Orient. *Champlevé* (shahm-pluh-*vey*), enamel applied to a design carved into the metal, is the reverse of cloisonné. When the enamel is suspended between metal strips without a backing, like a tiny stained glass window, it is called *plique-à-jour* (pleek-ah-*jur*). Transparent enamel applied over a relief carving is called *basse-taille* (*baz*-tahye).

Grisaille (griz-*aye*-uh) is enameling done in blacks, whites, and grays; *taille d'épergne* (*tah*-ye-*deh*-purn) is engraved ornamentation filled with blue or black enamel.

Lacquer refers to a number of natural and synthetic finishings. In reference to metalwork, however, it refers to an unfused organic enamel which is not fired. Lacquer is most appropriately used on relatively large surfaces—such as a broad, flat pin—where the danger of chipping is minimized. Lacquer scratches more easily than enamel because of its unfused nature.

Paillons (pay-*ohns*) are tiny ornaments stamped from very thin sheets of gold that decorate some enamelwork. They often take the form of flowers, stars, or birds.

5

Gemstones

Gemstone. Gem. Jewel. The words are used interchangeably by most people, but to jewelers they have specialized meanings. A *gemstone* is material (known in the trade as *rough*) that can be cut and polished into a gem. Most gemstones look fairly nondescript until they're cut and polished at the hands of a skilled lapidary (or, in the case of diamonds, a skilled diamond cutter). Gemstones are usually, but not always, minerals—upscale versions of beach pebbles and driveway gravel. A few, such as pearls and amber, once were living tissue.

When a gemstone has been cut and polished, it becomes a *gem*. When a gem is set for display, usually in precious metal, it's called a *jewel*.

Of the hundred-plus elements in the earth's crust, only some two dozen combine with one another in such a way as to produce stones of beauty sufficient to raise armies and of sturdiness equal to the wear and tear of cocktail parties. Even then, material chemically identical to a fine gemstone is not necessarily valuable in the commercial sense of the term. Mediocre pearls and low-grade diamonds are the real thing, and may acquire quite a bit of sentimental value in a family, but as far as resale value goes, they're little more than pricey costume jewelry.

This is because chemical makeup is only one criterion a stone must meet to be considered gem-class material. The other criteria are color, reaction to light, size, hardness, durability (which is not the same as hardness), rarity, and the degree to which the stone approaches the ideal. Occasionally a gem's pedigree is a factor (whether it belonged to Elizabeth Taylor, for instance, or was involved in a historical event); and stones, like anything else, go in and out of fashion.

A note of caution: be wary of any gemstone

that has a geographical name attached to it, unless its point of origin can be documented. This is because many lesser gemstones, especially the quartz varieties and garnets, have been sold in the past as if they were more valuable stones. Unless a "Burma ruby" can be proved to be from Burma, for example, you shouldn't have to pay the price a genuine Burmese ruby would command. A Herkimer diamond isn't a bargain-priced diamond that just lacks the status of one mined in South Africa; it's good old rock crystal, a form of transparent quartz.

COLOR

The difference between an expensive citrine and a less expensive amethyst is a minute quantity of trace element; the two gemstones are identical varieties of quartz. Rubies and sapphires are, except for trace elements, identical forms of corundum. Color has a great impact on the eventual price of such gemstones; the most costly form of turquoise is a clear, deep robin's-egg blue. The more closely the color of turquoise resembles the blue-green most people associate with it, the less valuable it is.

Although trace elements affect a number of gemstones, others are relatively free from such variations. Peridot, for example, is always some shade of green. This is because green is the inevitable result of the compound formed by the iron, manganese, and silica of which it is composed. Similarly, azurite is invariably bright blue.

Gemstone color also can be affected by dyes, heat or chemical treatment, or irradiation. Some of these processes result in permanent color change; others give results that may last for many years but that ultimately fade. In general, an untreated gemstone has more value—and a correspondingly higher price tag—than a gem of comparable size and quality that has been color-enhanced. How to tell the difference? Ask. A reputable jeweler will not only give you a written statement as to whether the gemstone has been subjected to color treatment but will also inform you whether such treatment is permanent or only long-lasting.

CRYSTALLINE STRUCTURE

Except for opal and obsidian, which look like freeform blobs under a microscope, all mineral-based gemstones are composed of *crystals*. This means that when the atoms combined to form the gemstone, they followed certain specific patterns which were repeated again and again, causing the stone to grow in size. The patterns are called *crystal lattices,* and are different for each species of gemstone.

Gemologists, diamond cutters, and lapidaries have to understand crystalline structure because a gem shows its true color only when its cut is based on that structure. *You* have to know about crystal structure so that you'll be able to look through a jeweler's loupe and make some intelligent decisions about whether a stone is worth a trip to the jewelry store for an appraisal. You certainly don't need to know as much as a lapidary, but a few facts will be very helpful.

Crystals come in six atomic arrangements (see Figure 2), which bear a direct relationship to the traditional shapes in which certain stones are cut.

The crystal shapes are:

Cubic: diamond, spinel, garnet
Hexagonal: ruby, emerald, quartz
Tetragonal: zircon
Orthorhombic: topaz, peridot, chrysoberyl
Monoclinic: the jades
Triclinic: turquoise

It's an oversimplification, but one could say that a diamond cut in one of the classic brilliant forms is basically a faceted cube.

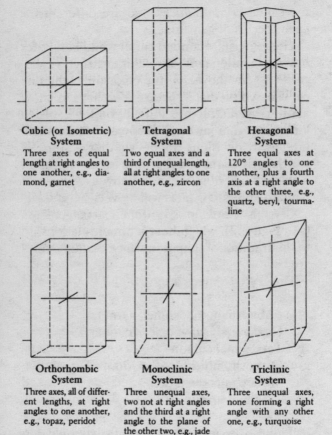

Cubic (or Isometric) System

Three axes of equal length at right angles to one another, e.g., diamond, garnet

Tetragonal System

Two equal axes and a third of unequal length, all at right angles to one another, e.g., zircon

Hexagonal System

Three equal axes at 120° angles to one another, plus a fourth axis at a right angle to the other three, e.g., quartz, beryl, tourmaline

Orthorhombic System

Three axes, all of different lengths, at right angles to one another, e.g., topaz, peridot

Monoclinic System

Three unequal axes, two not at right angles and the third at a right angle to the plane of the other two, e.g., jade

Triclinic System

Three unequal axes, none forming a right angle with any other one, e.g., turquoise

FIGURE 2.   Crystal structures.

CUT

A *facet* is a flat, polished surface set at an angle to another flat, polished surface. Transparent gems are faceted because facets catch light and bounce it around inside the stone before returning it to the eye. Diamonds and zircon are especially good at intensifying the light as it bounces. When the light flashes from a gem, the flash is called *fire*.

There's a whole vocabulary of words attached to faceted stones (see Figure 3). The upper part is called the *crown;* the large center facet in the crown is the *table*. The lower portion of the stone, where it begins to decrease in width, is the *pavilion;* the very tiny facet at the pavilion's bottom (corresponding to the table) is the *culet*. The widest part of the stone, separating crown and pavilion, is the *girdle*.

Gems that are not transparent are usually not faceted. Some, such as agate and bloodstone, are often cut with wide, flat surfaces to emphasize their patterns. Others, such as opals and lapis, are more often cut *en cabochon,* a French term that comes from an old word for "cabbage." Cabochon-cut stones usually have a rounded top and a flat bottom, although occasionally both sides will be rounded. Figure 4 illustrates these gemstone cuts.

Gemstones also can be carved. A raised

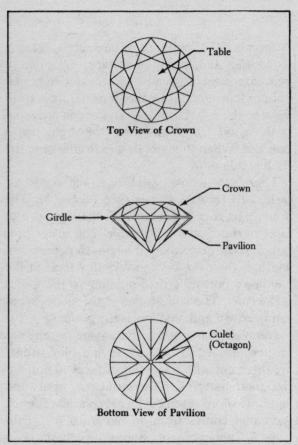

FIGURE 3. Parts of a faceted gemstone (brilliant cut).

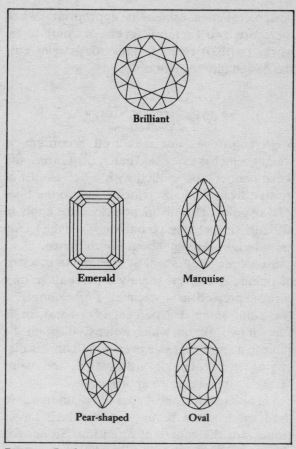

FIGURE 4. Popular gemstone cuts (viewed from the top).

design, called a *cameo,* is appropriate when there are two or more layers of color to be worked with. A reverse cameo, or *intaglio,* cuts the design into the stone.

WEIGHT AND SIZE

Most gemstones are measured according to weight, which is expressed in terms of *carats,* the word deliberately spelled with a "c" to distinguish it from the karat which refers to the fineness of gold. (This distinction does not apply in all English-speaking countries, however.) One carat weighs .2 gram, about ¹⁄₁₄₀th ounce.

Sometimes stones will be referred to in terms of points. A point is merely a percentage of a carat expressed as a decimal. For example, a two-point stone is 2 percent of a carat, or .2 ("point two") carat, which weighs .002 gram. To refer to a stone that size even as a "chip" is dignifying it beyond all justification; the word "flake" would be more appropriate.

Tiny pieces of stone, generally diamonds, are used to decorate mountings in which larger stones are the center of attention. Stones for this purpose are cut as small as 400 to the carat. In the best jewelry, these stones are not merely scrap left from cutting a larger stone; they're fully faceted. Some have almost as many facets as a brilliant-cut diamond—57 surfaces in a *full-cut stone,* 33 in a *Swiss-cut,* 17 in a *single-cut.* When these smaller stones are placed in a setting, they are called *melee* (pronounced *mel-ee*). Because there's a considerable amount of labor involved in cutting these tiny stones, their small size does not translate into small price.

Other designations for mass settings of tiny gemstones include *pavé* (pronounced pah-*vay*) which describes stones set side by side, flush with the surface, with no metal showing between them. Think of them as tiny, exquisitely expensive paving stones. *Baguettes,* usually cut larger than 50 to the carat, are shaped like tiny faceted rectangles.

Except when stones of the same species and similar cut are being compared, a gemstone's carat weight is not necessarily an indication of size. A one-carat diamond, for example, is considerably larger than a one-carat sapphire. This is because a diamond is much less dense than a sapphire—that is, a diamond's molecules are farther apart than a sapphire's. Figure 5 shows comparable sizes and weights of diamonds.

Not all stones are measured by carats. The ones that are so measured include diamonds, the beryls (emeralds and aquamarines), and corundums (rubies and sapphires), spinels, topaz, tourmalines, and zircons. Pearls sometimes are referred to in terms of carats, but more frequently they're sold by diameter (diameter is measured in millimeters) or by the grain (a grain is equal to ½0th gram). There are four pearl grains to the carat. Most quartz stones and opals are sold by the millimeter, and all but the most exceptional stones are cut to standard calibrated sizes to fit into standard settings.

At one time it would have been safe to say that the finest stones were sold by the carat and others by the millimeter, but that has changed in the United States in recent generations. Part of the reason for the change is to increase the market for less rare but nevertheless lovely stones, part is to educate the public to the fact

	Carat Weight			
	1/2	1	2	4
Emerald Cut	▭	▭	▭	▭
Marquise Cut	◇	◇	◇	◇
Brilliant Cut	◉	◉	◉	◉

FIGURE 5. Gemstone sizes (comparable sizes and weights of diamonds).

that a high-grade amethyst is usually a wiser purchase than a mediocre diamond.

STRENGTH

Strength is an important factor in a stone's value. *Hardness* is the best-known characteristic of strength, but there are several others. *Friability* measures a stone's resistance to crumbling. *Toughness* (or *tenacity*) measures resistance to fracture. The toughest stones are not necessarily the hardest. The jades, for example, rank highest in toughness for stones usually cut en cabochon, yet on the scale of hardness (see Table 2 in the Appendix), they rank only in the mid-sixes.

Hardness is measured by which stone scratches which. This is not a test to try at home! Hardness testing is usually done on the uncut stone at the time of assay (when, for example, you bring that pretty rock to a jeweler on the chance that the red stuff is ruby instead of garnet). Hardness tests also can be performed after a gem is mounted, but it's important that it be done by a professional, on an inconspicuous part of the stone. These techniques are covered in some detail in Chapter 12.

Gemstone hardness is ranked on the *Mohs scale,* a 10-point listing named after the scientist who first formulated it. The Mohs scale reflects only the order of increasing hardness, not the degree. The difference in degree of hardness between a diamond, at 10, and a ruby, at 9, is greater than the difference between 9 and 1 (between ruby, for instance, and talc, a loosely bound mineral that needs little encouragement to fall apart into bath powder).

OTHER CRITERIA

Rarity and the degree to which the stone approaches perfection reinforce one another in determining a gem's value. Although diamonds obviously are scarcer than quartz, they are not quite as scarce as the group that controls their marketing would have you believe.

On the other hand, diamonds of truly magnificent quality *are* rare, and discoveries of genuinely flawless stones of any remarkable size are events of a generation. Rubies and emeralds occur in nature even less frequently than diamonds; in stones of more than five carats, both are considerably more valuable than diamonds of comparable size and quality, with rubies having the edge.

Although jewelry is somewhat affected by the caprice of fashion, there hasn't been a drastic switch in gemstone popularity since the Western world came out of mourning for Prince Albert after his widow, Queen Victoria, died in 1903. (Victoria had carried mourning beyond the call of duty, by several decades. When her fun-loving son ascended the throne and inaugurated the Edwardian era, suppliers of onyx and jet were left with a considerable inventory.) Today, any quality stone given reasonable care will serve you well for dozens of years. If your heirs don't care for your taste, they can always have the gem remounted.

The historical value of a given piece of jewelry is a consideration in determining value, but if you are on the verge of popping for a stone associated with a tragic princess or a medieval intrigue, investigate the credentials of the seller twice and then hie thyself to the nearest curator of decorative arts for further advice. Discussion of such a purchase is beyond the scope of this book.

A DO-IT-YOURSELF APPRAISAL

If, however, the only history connected with a gemstone is a family one, there are some simple tests you can perform at home to decide whether the loot is better off in a safe-deposit box or your kids' toy chest.

The first thing to do is to take the stone's temperature. You can do this by touching it to your lip or your tongue. Glass warms up almost instantly, but with the exception of opal, mineral-based crystals will remain cool for quite a while. If it does turn out to be glass, don't discard it on the spot. Classic *paste* is made with a heavy, transparent flint glass that can do a credible job of passing for a good gemstone; the best is highly polished and has sharp, precisely cut edges. Paste can be quite lovely in its own right, and the correct response to nosy questions is "I don't really know how much it's worth. It was great-grandmama's, and I've just never gotten around to having it appraised."

Paste gets its name because its components are mixed together in semi-liquid form, or paste, as opposed to glassmaking techniques that use a dry mix. Paste of low quality has rounded facets, the result of being formed by molding rather than by hand cutting; often telltale air bubbles are trapped in molded paste as the melted glass cools.

Another way to tell if the gem in question is paste or mineral is to try to scratch glass with it. This is not recommended, however, because it might damage the facet of a harder, though genuine, stone. A safer way is the water test: a drop of water will hold its shape on clean genuine stone, like raindrops on a freshly waxed automobile hood; on clean glass, however, water drops quickly spread out.

If your preliminary tests tell you that the clear, sparkling stones in Aunt Kitty's hideous brooch aren't glass after all, don't plan on paying off the mortgage with the proceeds just yet. All clear, fiery minerals are not diamonds. Quartz crystal (the true rhinestone) and zircon are also possibilities. If the fire is only moderate, it's probably crystal. If there's a lot, it *could* be diamond, but it also could be zircon, or cubic zirconia if the piece is fairly modern. If you have access to a jeweler's loupe, try looking through a larger stone to the back facets. If they have a single edge, it's a diamond. A double edge means zircon. Knowing how Aunt Kitty loved to put on airs, you suspect the thing's probably zircon, but take it to a jeweler to be sure.

The setting is another key to the probable worth of a piece. If a transparent stone is set in prongs, it's more likely to be genuine than if it's glued to the setting, which indicates costume jewelry. If an opaque stone is held in the setting by a collar of metal, called a *bezel,* it could go either way.

Pearls are tricky. There is no easy way for the non-professional to detect the natural from the cultured. Simulated (imitation) pearls are another story, however. Any pearl that got its start in a shellfish, whether through an act of God or the intervention of a technician, feels rough as you draw it (gently!) across the front of your teeth. Imitations usually feel smooth. This test is not universally foolproof, because some imitations are textured, but it's a place to start.

If the gem in question is supposed to be jade, try to scratch it with a penknife in an inconspicuous place, perhaps the interior of a bangle or the back of an earring. If it's imitation, chances are it will scratch.

If the stone has been doctored to appear better than it is, you might not be successful in detecting the alteration. Heat is used to improve the color of aquamarines and to turn amethysts into citrines. Turquoise, jade, agate, and onyx can be dyed. The pavilion of a yellowish diamond can be touched up with violet dye so that the entire stone appears colorless to the untrained eye. A black backing can help the color display of a weak opal. All of these practices can be guarded against when purchasing a stone by insisting on the right documentation, but with a gem you already own, an expert's help may be needed to detect them.

More readily detectable are *doublets* and *triplets,* two or more layers of stone fused together to create the appearance of a single stone (see Figure 6). A very thin slice of opal, fronted with cabochon-cut quartz, can appear to be a substantial opal. Doublets and triplets can be detected by closely examining the side of the gem with a magnifying glass or jeweler's loupe.

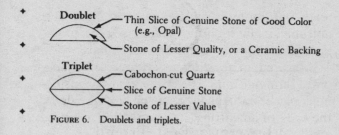

FIGURE 6. Doublets and triplets.

Imitation or doctored stones should not be confused with synthetic gems, which are the real McCoy even though they grew in a laboratory instead of the bowels of the earth. While not as valuable in absolute terms as the rarer natural gems, the differences are next to impossible for the non-professional to detect, or for the professional without a close examination. Almost the only giveaways in a social situation are the too-perfect star sapphire (natural ones are fuzzy, and slightly off-center) and rubies owned by anyone with an annual income of less than six figures.

6

A Diamond Is a
Jeweler's Best Friend

Ask the average jewelry store customer to tell
you three things about sapphires or cat's eyes,
and you're likely to hear nothing beyond the
color. But everybody has plenty to say about
diamonds:

1. They're a form of coal that's been under
   enormous pressure for billions of years.

2. They're so expensive because they're so
   rare.

3. A diamond engagement ring is always a good investment because you can always sell it if hard times befall you, and it always increases in value.

4. The bigger a diamond, the better.

However, as your mother used to tell you, "everybody" is not necessarily right all of the time. Consider the following.

In the early 1980s, the South African cartel that controls the vast majority of the world's diamond supply sharply reduced the number of stones it released to the world market. The reason for the cutback was not a sudden dropoff in the number of diamonds that were being mined. Rather, it was a careful maneuver to keep prices up, as high interest rates cut down on demand.

The strategy was only partly successful. At one point in 1987, a top-quality stone that would have sold for $55,000 a carat seven years earlier cost only $14,800 a carat, a bargain-basement price until you consider that only two years earlier, in 1985, it would have sold for a mere $8,500 a carat.

Now it must be realized that the diamonds most affected were the absolute top-of-the-line stones, the one percent more likely to be purchased by investors for their portfolios rather than young men for their brides-to-be. Jewelry prices, particularly for the smaller stones (less than half a carat) that make up the vast majority of the retail trade, fluctuated less dramatically. But fluctuate they did, and the chronology illustrates an aspect of the business not necessarily appreciated by the average jewelry store customer.

HOW RARE IS RARE?

Diamonds aren't as rare as most people think. They certainly aren't the rarest of the traditional gemstones; both rubies and emeralds are rarer, and in comparable stones of five or more carats, a ruby or an emerald would easily surpass a diamond in cost.

True, diamonds are less abundant than rock crystal or garnets, and there are only a dozen places in the world where they are mined in commercial quantities. However, those locations (Zaire, South Africa, Botswana, Ghana, Namibia, Angola, Sierra Leone, Tanzania, the Soviet Union, Venezuela, Brazil, and Australia) yielded nearly 90 million carats worth of diamonds in 1986, and if only ten percent of those carats were of gem quality, that's about nine million one-carat rings or an untold number of smaller pieces, and nine million of anything is a fairly hefty inventory. A good portion of the non-gem quality finds its way into jewelry as well, as the sort of thing high school sweethearts can afford.

Aside from the production costs, which admittedly are not small, what makes diamonds costly is the law of supply and demand. As it happens, De Beers, the cartel that controls the market, has a better handle on the supply than does Mother Nature, who is forever yawning in some godforsaken corner of the world and yielding up another mine. The usual scenario is for De Beers to buy up the output of the new mine to prevent a flood of new stones from depressing prices. The current estimate is that De Beers, through its Central Selling Organization, controls 80 percent of the world diamond market, including most production in the non-Communist world, and some of the Soviet Union's as well.

To this, add markups by diamond cutters, wholesalers, and retailers, and you find yourself with one pricey piece of carbon.

BASIC DIAMOND INFORMATION

Form and Substance

A diamond is composed almost exclusively of carbon whose atoms have bonded in such a way as to form isometric, or equal-sided, crystals. Think of ice cubes, if you can stand the pun. In one sense, diamond is a cousin of coal (and graphite—pencil lead—as well) because of the carbon content, but diamond atoms have arranged very differently, with very different results. This, however, is where the "diamonds are coal" legend comes from; like many myths, it is an oversimplified but easy-to-remember version of the real story. A contributing factor is that deposits of diamond-containing rock are sometimes found in coal fields.

Diamonds are the hardest naturally occurring substance yet discovered, but contrary to another bit of popular wisdom, they're not immune to damage. Hardness refers to how well a gem resists scratches, not fractures (see the hardness and toughness scales in Tables 2 and 3 in the Appendix). Given the right kind of shock, any diamond will crack or chip along the lines of its crystal lattice; in fact, that's how a gemstone can be cut in the first place, by taking advantage of its tendency to fracture along definite, predictable lines.

Most diamonds found in nature are either off-color (brown, gray, or yellowish) or so imperfect that their defects are obvious to the naked eye. Stones that are cracked or have carbon spots, cloudy interiors, or misshapen crystals are sold to industry, where a gem's performance on the edge of a saw wheel is more important than how it handles light.

Some industrial-grade stones do find their way to the jewelry counter, however; they're the ones you see advertised as "genuine one-carat diamonds for the unheard-of low price of $249.99—easy credit terms."

How Diamonds Are Graded

There are several systems for grading diamonds, all of them based on the "Four Cs"— color, cut, clarity, and carat weight.

COLOR: Unlike a diamond's cousins coal and graphite, jewelry-quality diamonds are transparent, and most have some degree of tint, usually yellow, caused by minute quantities of trace elements in the crystal. Truly colorless stones are very rare, and very costly. Stones that have a pleasing tint are called "fancy colored diamonds" or "fancies," and range in color from true yellow (not a liability in a stone of otherwise exceptional quality) on through the rainbow. Matched sets of natural fancy stones can command wonderfully high prices in a booming market.

The color of off-color stones can usually be improved through radiation treatment; such gemstones are called irradiated diamonds. Reputable jewelers will disclose irradiation at the time of sale; ideally, the information will be given voluntarily, but you may have to ask. *Do ask,* and get a written statement from the dealer if he or she asserts the color is natural.

There are four systems for grading color that are, or have been, used in North America. Two of the older systems depend on naked-eye judgments by diamond experts. One dates from the early days of the South African diamond industry, and has such picturesque levels as river (absolutely colorless), top Wesselton (named after a mine), Wesselton, top crystal, crystal, top cape, cape, light yellow, yellow.

Another dated system preserves the cape and yellow categories at the bottom, but designates only three top rankings: blue white (top), fine white, and commercial white. Few contemporary jewelers use either of these systems today, but you may find reference to them in old appraisals or the inventories of safe-deposit boxes.

Newer systems are more scientific. A system used by the American Gem Society (a national association of jewelry retailers and suppliers) grades diamonds by comparison against known master color grading stones. Grades 0, 1, and 2 will be colorless to the naked eye; Grades 3 and 4 will show some tint if you look for it; Grades 5 through 10 are better left alone.

The Gemological Institute of America (the

education, research, and testing center for the industry) and its Gem Trade Laboratories use a letter system which compares a diamond to a set of standard color stones. D is the absolute top of the line; E, F, G, H, and I are colorless to the untrained eye; J, K, L will look colorless when mounted except in the larger stones, and stones beyond M become increasingly yellowish to downright dim.

When buying a diamond, it's perfectly acceptable to ask to compare the stone you're considering with whichever set of master color stones your jeweler has. Be certain to check that the master stones are actually diamonds and not mere representations in glass or other material.

CLARITY: The value of a diamond also depends on how free it is from internal inclusions, such as misoriented internal crystals, tiny interior breaks in the stone, tiny gas pockets or bits of other minerals, and external blemishes, such as tiny nicks, scratches, or marks from the polishing wheel. These inclusions and blemishes affect how the diamond handles light, thus diminishing a stone's value.

Flawless, or perfect, is the top-of-the-line designation, but (with apologies to English teachers who insist that something is either perfect or it is not) there are degrees to this perfection. Some systems for grading use three or five grades for clarity; others use as many as eleven. The American Gem Society uses a grading scale of 0 to 10; the Gemological Institute of America uses a system that recognizes nine grades: flawless (or perfect), very very slightly imperfect (mercifully abbreviated VVS_1), VVS_2, very slightly imperfect/VS_1, VS_2, slightly imperfect/ SI, SI_2, imperfect/I, I_2. (Instead of "imperfect," some jewelers prefer the term "included.")

CUT AND SHAPE: Diamond cutting is a highly skilled art, and not every diamond bears close inspection. Both AGS and GIA offer cut assessments which evaluate facet execution, angles, and placements of the facets on a diamond; such an evaluation is worth asking for in order to avoid buying a miscut gem.

Diamonds once were cut to preserve their size, but today size takes a backseat to beauty. A diamond usually is cut to make the most of its powers to disperse light, with the 58-facet round brilliant cut being the preferred shape for maximum "fire," that flash of rainbow-colored light that results when the stone acts as a prism to separate light into its component colors. The venerable fashion maxim that colored stones are to be worn in daylight, and diamonds at night, has its origin in the fact that diamonds flash the most by candlelight.

Other popular shapes for diamonds are the

marquise, emerald, and pear shapes (although the pear looks more like a teardrop than a Bartlett). As noted in Chapter Five, small stones frequently are used in great numbers to set off a larger stone.

CARAT WEIGHT: Bigger is better only when comparing stones of comparable quality. Obviously, a four-carat, D flawless round brilliant cut is of much better quality than a four-carat H VS_2. Pricing per carat usually follows the "rule of square,"

Base price of a one-carat stone × Number of carats^2

This means that if a one-carat stone costs $1,000 retail, a two-carat stone of comparable quality will cost $1,000 × 2 × 2, or $4,000. A four-carat stone will cost $1,000 × 4 × 4, or $16,-000.

Regardless of which grading system is being used, the price differences between grades of diamond are significant. Very few stones meet the top standards; if they are free from internal flaws, there may be imperfections due to poor faceting. A difference of one degree in the angle of a facet can make a detectable difference to an expert; a difference of two degrees is obvious to a non-professional but practiced observer. In all but the finest stores, a less-than-precise cut is the rule rather than the exception, because the public's untutored thirst for diamonds can be satisfied by stones that jewelers purchase at cut-rate prices and mark up for a very nice profit margin.

DIAMONDS AS INVESTMENTS

A stone of great perfection has a high resale value, one that will usually increase with time. The average engagement ring, however, increases only nominally in value from year to year, and that value is more likely to be based on an estimate for insurance purposes, rather than for resale purposes. In other words, what it will cost you to replace a diamond that drops out of its setting and rolls into the bathroom drain is likely to be much more than you'd get by taking the ring in to a jeweler and asking that it be sold as "estate" jewelry. That's because you have to replace it at retail, but the jeweler won't pay you retail costs when he or she can get a comparable stone at wholesale prices.

From the standpoint of annual yield, therefore, your money usually is better off in a high-interest savings instrument. This is not to downgrade the emotional bond an engagement ring symbolizes, but it's important to be realistic about what you're purchasing. For the price a reasonably affluent couple pays for a reasonably impressive engagement diamond, they could get a superior stone in a less popular gem, such as an aquamarine or a pearl. You're paying for tradition, not for a hedge against financial ruin.

DIAMOND TRIVIA

For what it's worth, and that's a great deal, the largest cut diamond in the world is the Great Star of Africa, a teardrop-shaped stone weighing in at 530.2 carats. It's set in the King's Royal Scepter, part of the British Crown Jewels. The second largest is also among the Crown Jewel collection in the Tower of London: the Cullinan II, at 317.4 carats. It's in the Imperial State Crown. The third largest is the Jubilee diamond, cut for Queen Victoria in 1879; it weighs a bit over 245 carats and is in a private collection.

It's no accident that these fabulous stones are associated with the British Empire. Diamonds became a world-class industry during Victoria's reign.

A number of gemstones are called diamonds but aren't the real thing. A *Herkimer diamond,* for example, is rock crystal from Herkimer County in New York state. *Ceylon diamonds* are colorless *zircon,* a fiery stone that can pass for diamonds but rank only 7 on the Mohs scale. An *Alaska diamond* is hematite, a brilliant black opaque crystal often used as a substitute for jet. Few of these could pass for a diamond on close examination. Synthetic diamonds, on the other hand, require an expert to tell them from the natural article. The most prevalent synthetic is called *cubic zirconia,* which has all but replaced zircon.

7

Rubies, Emeralds, and
Close Relatives

In colors other than red and green:
ruby is sapphire;
emerald, aquamarine.

Ask any reasonably well-educated person to
name precious stones that aren't diamonds, and
it's likely that rubies and emeralds will top the
list. From fairy-tale troves to the legendary jewels of long-defunct monarchs, rubies and emeralds have a longer history of symbolizing luxury
and great wealth than any other gemstone.

But for all that, popular knowledge about rubies and emeralds is fairly thin. In part, this is
because they don't have a high-powered "ru-

bies/emeralds are forever" marketing push behind them. There's a good reason for that; high-quality, high-carat rubies and emeralds are much scarcer than comparable diamonds, and correspondingly more costly. Suppliers don't have to create a market for their output; there isn't that much output to begin with. For this reason, synthetic stones are especially available in these four gem categories.

Few people outside the industry realize that rubies and sapphires are the same material, a hexagonal crystal called corundum, or that emeralds and aquamarines, also hexagonal, are both beryls. The difference is in the sort of trace elements that were trapped in the crystal as it was formed deep in the earth. Chromium turns corundum red and beryl, green. Without significant chromium, gem-quality corundum is not a ruby but a sapphire, colored deep blue in its most favored form. Beryl without chromium is almost any color but red or green; aquamarine is the usual designation for gem-quality beryl.

CORUNDUM

Corundum ranks right below diamond on the Mohs scale, making it one of the world's hardest naturally occurring substances. Corundum doesn't have the flashing fire of diamonds, but most transparent varieties are brilliant cut, which gives them a certain sparkle. Nontransparent varieties, such as the star sapphires, are cabochon cut.

Red corundum is called *ruby,* and comes in several shades. The most valuable, historically known by the unappetizing though highly descriptive name of pigeon's blood, is a deep blue-red and once was found mainly in Burma. Rubies with a brownish cast are generally from Thailand, and those with a violet cast from Sri Lanka (the former Ceylon). True rubies also are found in Montana, although that state is becoming more noted for its sapphires, and North Carolina.

Genuine rubies are sometimes called *oriental rubies* to distinguish them from red gemstones of lesser value. *Spinel* is one of the look-alikes; often the difference can't be detected except by a trained gemologist using a microscope. This explains why it took until 1783 for someone to discover the difference. Several famous "rubies" in royal collections are actually spinel, including the Black Prince's Ruby in the British Crown Jewels.

Balas ruby is pink to red spinel. *Arizona rubies, cape rubies,* or *Australian rubies* usually are garnet. *Siberian rubies* are rubellite, a red variety of tourmaline. *Brazil rubies* are often pink topaz. Although beautiful gems in their own right, they are not true rubies and should be priced accordingly.

Corundum that isn't ruby is *sapphire,* usually thought of as blue but also occurring as gray, yellow, pale pink, orange, violet, green, brown, and colorless. A medium cornflower blue is the most valuable color. Small amounts of iron and titanium in the crystal account for the color.

Most sapphire also contains tiny particles of another mineral, usually *rutile,* which gives the stone a soft, whitish sheen called *silk.* When these inclusions have arranged themselves in regular patterns, they cause the optical phenomenon known as *asterism,* which is the "star" of star sapphires and star rubies. The stars in natural star sapphires are a bit fuzzy; too well-defined a star is a sign that the gem is manufactured rather than natural. An imperfectly formed star changes the phenomenon to *chatoyancy,* and the gem is known as a corundum *cat's eye.*

Sapphire is found in many of the same geographical locations as ruby. Burma and Thailand produce deep blue stones. The sought-after cornflower blues traditionally came from the Kashmir province of India, but a deposit of stones in the less-than-exotic location of Yugo Gulch, Montana, has had an impact on the market in recent years. Violet stones tend to come from Sri Lanka.

Most colored stones on the market today are color-enhanced to some degree. Heat, chemicals, and radiation are used, often at the mine sites themselves, to improve the color or smooth out minor flaws. Reputable jewelers will tell you this if you ask, but often *only* if you ask, despite an FTC requirement that color enhancement be voluntarily disclosed. Jewelry industry organizations have recently put out guidelines for such disclosure, so it may be more forthcoming in the future. Because some enhancements are less permanent than others, such treatment can have an impact on a gem's asking price.

An exception to color enhancement seems to be the Montana sapphires, which come with written guarantees that the stones haven't been treated with heat or chemicals.

BERYL

The beryls include emerald and aquamarine and the less familiar morganite and heliodor. Emeralds weighing more than ten carats are exceedingly rare, and flawlessness is nonexistent. Therefore, the quality of the stone is measured in terms of relative flawlessness.

Compared with diamonds, the beryl gems are significantly more fragile. On the hardness scale they rank only 7.5 to 8, and they're close to the bottom on the durability scale. What little fire the beryls have is shown to best advantage in the so-called emerald cut (also known as a "step cut"), an oblong shape with as many facets as a brilliant cut.

Deep green beryl is called *emerald.* Colombia historically produced the best-quality emeralds in the largest quantity, but emeralds are also found in Russia, Norway, the Austrian Alps, India, and North Carolina. A recent discovery of genuine emeralds in Brazil may make that nation a major producer as well. Since color is about all the gem has going for it, the paler beryls aren't considered gem-quality emeralds.

As with most other precious stones, an adjective before the word "emerald" is a giveaway that the stone is not a true emerald, no matter how superficially it resembles the real thing. *Uralian emerald* is a garnet from the Ural Mountains of Russia. *Brazilian emerald,* not to be confused with the recent find noted above, usually is green tourmaline. An *evening emerald* is an outdated name for peridot.

Emeralds are manufactured commercially, and the synthetic stones are indistinguishable from the natural gem under normal lighting. However, under ultraviolet light, synthetic emeralds flouresce (glow) a deep red, while the natural gems do not.

No clear-cut legal standard exists for determining when a stone is an *aquamarine* rather than a pale emerald or light green beryl, but the term is usually applied to pale sea-blue beryl with a tendency toward green. Most aquamarine is mined in Brazil, and it's also found in Russia, Madagascar, and several places in the United States along the Appalachian and Rocky Mountain ranges.

Morganite is colored peach, rose, or pink, and natural (not color-enhanced) specimens are scarcer than aquamarine but more abundant than emerald. *Heliodor* is an uncommon golden yellow form of beryl.

8

The Fragile Jewels

Most gemstones are just that, gem *stones*. As such, they're pretty sturdy customers as long as they're not knocked about in a careless fashion. However, that's not the case with the fragile eight, most of which were once living things. Special care must be taken with amber, coral, ivory (whether it's the real thing or bone ivory), jet, opal, pearl, tortoise shell, and turquoise. These gems need special care to preserve their beauty and value.

AMBER

Amber is the fossilized version of the sticky resin that oozes out of a Christmas tree after a few days in a warm house. Amber jewelry is the costume jewelry of a bygone era, and today good antique amber commands prices comparable to new jewelry in other stones. Newly-crafted pieces are also sold in some places of the world that are close to amber deposits, such as resorts near the Baltic Sea and in the Dominican Republic.

Usually colored yellow, orange, or brown, amber also has a milky white form called *bone amber*. In all but the rarest pieces, genuine amber will contain inclusions—bits of moss, tiny twigs, even entire insects that were trapped in the resin as it oozed out of a tree hundreds of centuries ago. Unlike a diamond inclusion, an amber inclusion increases its value, and the more sharply defined the impurity, the more expensive the piece.

Amber can be faceted, cut en cabochon, or shaped into beads. It also can take other forms; the heroine of Jane Austen's *Mansfield Park* treasured an amber cross brought home by a seafaring brother. Before plastics were developed, the mouthpieces of gentlemen's smoking pipes were often made from amber.

Pressed amber, made from bits of genuine

amber that have been melted and reshaped, is considerably less valuable than the original material. This processing can be detected by looking through a jeweler's loupe for flow lines in the material.

In your great-grandmother's time, it was safe to rely on static electricity for determining if a piece of amber was genuine; if the amber picked up tiny bits of paper after being rubbed briskly across a piece of wool, it was the real thing. Although this test is now obsolete because many plastic imitations will do the same thing, plastic "amber" can usually be detected because it's too perfect. It lacks the cloudiness and inclusions that characterize true amber.

Amber should be cleaned only with a dry, soft cloth.

CORAL

Gem-quality coral is found in several of the seven seas. The most highly prized is the dark red variety found off the coasts of Tunisia and Algeria. A black coral and a less valuable pink variety come from the ocean around Hawaii, and a blue coral is found in the Indian Ocean as well as parts of the Pacific. Dyed coral should be purchased with caution, because the treatment is not always stable.

Coral, which in its raw form is the many-branched remains of colonies of tiny sea creatures, is carved into beads, cameos, and other ornamental forms. It ranks only 3.5 on the Mohs scale, and therefore should be protected from abrasion. It can be safely cleaned with a damp cloth, but must never be subjected to commercial jewelry cleaner or any acid substance.

IVORY

Ivory is, to mix a metaphor, a hornet's nest. Ivory from Asian elephants can't be legally imported into the United States because the Asian elephant is protected under the Endangered Species Act. The African elephant, however, is merely "threatened," so its tusks can be legally imported if the importer has the proper license and documentation. Of course, the distinction between a species being "endangered" and being merely "threatened" is a fine one, and a good case can be made for forgoing the purchase of all elephant ivory (except for genuine antique pieces) on moral grounds alone. From a purely practical standpoint, it makes sense to avoid overseas purchases of ivory unless you are very, very sure of your dealer *and* can obtain documentation that will satisfy the customs inspector back in the United States.

Because of the restrictions and ambiguity surrounding the legal status of ivory made from genuine elephant tusks, most new "ivory" on the market is *bone ivory,* which comes from a variety of animals.

Elephant ivory, which now is found mainly in antique pieces, has a glossy, fatty look and is crosshatched with small, brown channels. Antique pieces have a mellow, beige patina. *Bone ivory,* on the other hand, is white or yellowish, with a dull surface. The bone comes from the larger animals, such as whale or hippopotamus, although as international whaling is outlawed, genuine new whalebone may become unobtainable. *Scrimshaw,* for instance, is decorative carving on whalebone (but be sure to get documentation that it actually *is* whalebone). Bone ivory also is made from the tusks of walrus, narwhal, and warthog. *Fossil ivory* is carved from the tusks of the extinct woolly mammoth. Another form of ivory, the least expensive, is *vegetable ivory,* which comes from the nut of certain palm trees.

No matter its source, all ivory will split if soaked in water. It can be cleaned with a cotton swab or soft cloth dampened in soapy water, but must be dried immediately. Should you insist on trying to whiten a piece of old ivory, dampen a swab or cloth in a weak solution of peroxide and water, increasing the strength of the solution until you see some results. When cleaning beads take special care not to get the string damp; a damp string will conduct moisture into the interior of the bead, expand the ivory cells, and cause the bead to split.

JET

Making a comeback after nearly a century of neglect, jet is showing up in costume jewelry as well as in more expensive pieces set in silver and 14K gold. Jet is a variety of coal that's a very dense, glossy black. Because of its internal structure, it's easily shaped into faceted beads. The real thing is heavy, feels warm to the touch and, like amber, will take a light electrical charge if rubbed on wool. It has a hardness between 3 and 4 on the Mohs scale.

It's difficult for the uninitiated to distinguish jet from black plastic imitations or glass, particularly when the material is mounted in an antique-looking setting. If you're buying from an antique dealer, be very certain of the dealer's reliability and knowledge, and insist on a written receipt guaranteeing that the piece is jet.

However, if you are knowledgeable and the dealer isn't, you can find yourself with a lovely and valuable brooch or necklace for a pittance.

Jet can be cleaned of powder, makeup

smudges, and finger marks by polishing it with a soft, dry cloth. Treat jet necklaces as you would any fine necklace, and have them restrung every few years to prevent deterioration of the string from body oils and perspiration.

OPAL

Precious opal, found in volcanic rock in several places around the world, is a quartz that doesn't form crystals. It resembles nothing so much as a hardened gel, a gel that in its most valuable form flashes iridescent colors as the stone catches the light from different angles. This particular kind of gemstone fire is known as *opalescence.*

Black opals, first discovered around the turn of the century, are a deep peacock blue or slate gray, with flashing red, yellow, and green lights. Most black opals come from Australia. *Harlequin opals,* from Czechoslovakia, are lighter in color. *Fire opals* have yellow, orange, or red bodies, and are found in New Zealand, Central America, Mexico, and the western United States. *Water opals* are bluish, white, pinkish, or greenish opals that display a good play of color. White opals that are nearly opaque and show only specks of fire are costume-jewelry quality, and come mainly from Japan.

Opals are almost always cut en cabochon. They range from 5 to 6.5 in hardness and must be protected from abrasion; this makes them poor choices for everyday rings or bracelets. The irony is that a frequently worn opal will be protected from another danger—cracking from excessive dryness—by the body's natural humidity. A light coating of baby oil may keep seldom-worn opals from cracking in dry climates and northern winters, although there are industry sources who say this sort of treatment is of questionable value. Clean opals only with the oft-recommended soft cloth.

PEARLS

It's common knowledge that pearls grow in oysters. Less commonly known is that most run-of-the-mill mollusks, including the common riverbank mussel found throughout the United States, also produce pearls, though admittedly of lower quality than those of the so-called pearl oyster.

A shellfish makes a pearl after some foreign object—a chip of shell, a snail, or a deliberately inserted pearl "seed"—finds its way into the soft interior of the animal. The shellfish neutralizes any damage the intruder might do to its soft, unprotected tissues by covering it with a substance called *nacre* (pronounced *nay*-ker). Nacre is secreted by the shellfish much as your eye secretes tears to protect itself against a stray eyelash. Unlike tears, however, nacre doesn't float the foreign body away; instead, it covers up the sharp edges, and keeps covering it and covering it for as long as the shellfish lives.

In oysters of the genus *Pinctada,* which range from the four-inch-long *fucata* to the foot-wide South Seas *maximas,* and in certain freshwater mussels, the nacre piles up in translucent, iridescent layers of such beauty that the pearl becomes a precious gem. Pearls approached by other varieties of mollusk usually, but not always, lack this high quality *orient,* or iridescent shimmer.

Cultured Pearls

When a pearl is formed by the oyster without any outside help, it's called a *natural pearl.* The vast majority of the pearls on the market today are *cultured pearls,* gems created by a process invented about 80 years ago, in which small beads formed from non-oyster shellfish are surgically implanted in oysters, along with a bit of live oyster tissue, at an oyster farm. The oysters are then returned to lake, river, or tank and allowed to live undisturbed for several years (ideally, a minimum of three) while they secrete nacre over the beads. The longer they have to work on the pearl, the thicker will be the nacre and the more durable the pearl. A *Mikimoto pearl* is a trade name for a pearl produced by the company formed by Kokichi Mikimoto, who received a Japanese patent for the cultured pearl process in 1908.

Most cultured pearls are produced in salt water, but not all. *Biwa pearls,* named for the Japanese lake where the process was perfected, are cultured freshwater pearls. They are produced by black mussels that are seeded with only a bit of oyster flesh, which is then absorbed into the pearl. A Biwa, therefore, is pearl through and through, whereas cultured pearls have a non-pearl core.

There is no easy way for the non-professional to detect a natural pearl from a cultured pearl, except by price. The vast majority of the pearls sold in the world today are cultured.

Pearl Imitations

Imitation pearls are sometimes sold forthrightly as fakes, but often advertisements disguise the true nature of such beads by referring to them as *faux pearls* ("faux" is French for "false"), *simulated pearls* (in hopes that you will confuse "simulated" with "cultured"), and *fun pearls* (to give the impression that these are the real thing, but in sizes and forms suitable for casual wear).

Most imitation pearls are glass or plastic beads that have been sprayed with a substance derived from fish scales. Natural and cultured pearls have a slight texture that can be detected by brushing the beads gently across one's teeth; however, some simulated pearls also are textured, so the tooth test is not fully reliable.

Mother-of-pearl is the iridescent lining of a mollusk (oyster or mussel) shell. In addition to seeding oysters, mother-of-pearl is used for small beads and inlay work.

Shape

A pearl's shape depends on where the pearl seed is implanted in the host shellfish. If the core is inserted deep into the animal's soft body area, the pearl will develop a round or pear shape. If it's inserted into muscle tissue, which expands and contracts as the animal digests its food, moves around, and is buffeted by waves, the stress will cause irregular growth and the result will be a *baroque pearl.* If the particle is placed between the shell and the animal's body, the nacre will form a solid dome over it and the finished pearl will be attached to the shell's interior. These pearls have a flat side when they are removed from the shell; they are called *Japan pearls, mabe pearls,* or *blister pearls.*

Color

Colors in natural pearls are influenced by the species of the host mollusk and by the area of the world in which it grows. Natural pearls from the Persian Gulf are cream-colored, the classic "pearl white." Australian natural pearls are white with a tinge of green or blue. Those from the Gulf of Panama are golden brown. Natural pearls from Mexico can be black or reddish brown. Those from Sri Lanka (Ceylon) have a pinkish tint.

The best cultured pearls are cream-colored, but many have a greenish tinge. As with many gems, the color often is modified through chemical means, but those which have not been augmented are more valuable, and more expensive.

Size

Pearls are measured either by weight or diameter. By weight, one pearl grain equals 50 milligrams, or one-quarter carat, and is a term generally reserved for natural pearls. Cultured pearls are weighed by the *momme,* a Japanese unit of weight that equals 18.75 carats or 75 grains (about 3.8 grams). *Seed pearls* (not to be confused with the mother-of-pearl cores that are "seeded" in the oyster) are by definition pearls that weigh less than one quarter grain. By diameter, pearls come in several general sizes: very small (less than three millimeters); small (to four-and-a-half millimeters); medium (to six millimeters); large (to eight millimeters), and very large (anything over eight millimeters). Very large can be very large indeed; some baroque pearls have weighed up to two-thirds of a pound.

How to Care for Pearls

A pearl is a soft gem, ranking 2.5 to 4.5 on the Mohs scale. The less expensive it is, the more fragile it is, because less expensive pearls have relatively thin layers of nacre from being harvested prematurely. The minimum thickness of nacre for a pearl you intend to keep for more than a few years of frequent wear should be .35 millimeters; .5 is better. Only the better jewelry stores will be willing to give you an assurance about nacre thickness; ask for documentation. Even high-quality cultured pearls won't last forever, but with proper care, you'll be able to pass them on to your grandchildren in good condition.

Proper care means protecting them from contact with rough fabric. If you like to wear your pearls with sweaters, this means angora or cashmere only; wear your "fun pearls" with your Shetlands. In the jewelry box, keep them from contact with other pieces of jewelry, ideally in a soft cloth bag. Do not, under any circumstances, keep your pearls in a plastic bag; this will seal out air and hasten deterioration.

If your pearls are so valuable they must be kept in a safe-deposit box while you're on vacation, or between parties, make sure the box does not sit beside one of the bank's heating or air conditioning ducts, and visit your pearls often so they can have a breath of fresh air.

After each wearing, wipe your pearls with a soft cloth or soft, dry chamois to remove body oil, makeup, and smoke film. Even if you have no place more exotic than the family room to go, wear them once a month anyway. The humidity from your body does them good. If you wear them on a regular basis, have them professionally cleaned every year to prevent dust, powder, and skin oils from accumulating in the bead holes. Have the beads restrung (and the clasp checked) the moment you notice the string stretching or looking dingy. And apply your perfume and hair spray before you take your pearls out of their bag or jewelry box.

TORTOISE SHELL

The hawksbill turtle, from whose shell came much lovely antique costume jewelry, dressing table appointments, and hair ornaments, is now protected under the Endangered Species Act. Therefore, it's illegal to import it in any form into this country, but some fine antique pieces are available. Make the dealer affirm in writing that the piece is genuine, and that if an appraiser discovers differently, you will be refunded your money. Then have it appraised immediately. Be particularly careful about buying pieces overseas; although the dealer may tell you there will be no problem taking it back to the United States, the customs inspector, who is not trying to make a living from the tourist trade, may have other ideas.

True tortoise shell is a translucent golden yellow with brown markings, and, like true amber, has an uneven color. If the piece looks too perfect, suspect plastic.

Care for a genuine piece as you would amber or ivory, cleaning it with only a soft cloth, keeping it out of the way of perfume and hair spray, and storing it in a separate bag of soft cloth.

TURQUOISE

Top-grade turquoise resists breakage and color loss. This cannot be overemphasized, because most turquoise on the market today, particularly that associated with Indian-style jewelry, is not gem-quality material. Despite the high prices, the stone in all but the finest authentic Native American pieces belongs in the costume jewelry category. The mines in the American Southwest and Mexico are just about played out, and soft, low-quality stone overlooked or thrown aside by miners the first time through the lode now is being recovered, dyed to improve its color, and impregnated with plastic to prevent breaking. These mine tailings are called *treated turquoise.*

Stabilized turquoise is a higher grade of stone that has good, but unstable, color. It's treated with plastic to prevent the color from changing in response to heat and light.

Dealers often will be honest about the fact that a stone has been treated or stabilized, but will try to make a virtue of necessity by saying these procedures are necessary for all turquoise. They aren't. The best turquoise—a deep sky blue—needs none of these procedures. Genuine gem-quality turquoise ranks between 5 and 6 on the Mohs scale and requires no special help to survive ordinary wear. It's just that turquoise of this quality is very hard to come by these days.

There are other pitfalls to turquoise, especially substitution. Even authentic Native American jewelry sometimes contains stones that look like turquoise, but aren't. This is because the maker was more interested in effect than chemistry. Frequent mimics are plastic, malachite, lapis, green chalcedony, azurite, agate, and quartz. (More information about buying American Indian jewelry is found in Chapter 11.)

Turquoise, even gem-quality turquoise, is porous and should be cleaned only with a soft, dry cloth. When polishing a silver mounting, be extraordinarily careful not to spatter the stone with water or any of the cleaning material. And never, never, *never* dip a silver mounting containing turquoise in a silver-cleaning solution . . . !

9

Other Gemstones:
Agate to Zircon

Once it was easy to make distinctions between gemstones. Diamonds, rubies, emeralds, sapphires, and some pearls were precious gems; everything else was "semiprecious," that is, nice but nothing to count on in lean times.

Those distinctions were a serious oversimplification. As you have learned in previous chapters, a high-quality aquamarine tops a poor diamond any day. A genuine citrine outclasses a poor ruby. There are opals, and then there are

opals. It all depends on the quality of the gemstone.

Most of the gemstones that formerly fell into
the semiprecious category are based on quartz,
a mineral composed of silicon and oxygen.
Quartz is one of the more abundant minerals in
the world, and comes in dozens of varieties, colors, and patterns with hundreds of different
names, many of them localized. Although it's
not necessary to go deeply into the science of
mineralogy, it is helpful to remember that
quartz comes in two basic forms. *Crystalline
quartz* forms large transparent masses that can
be several square feet in size. Amethyst and
rock crystal are crystalline forms of quartz.
Cryptocrystalline quartz, or *chalcedony,* forms
tiny crystals that produce translucent or opaque
masses, sometimes in bands of contrasting
color. Jasper, agate, and onyx are forms of cryptocrystalline quartz.

This chapter covers most of the quartz-based
gemstones, as well as other gemstone material.
For convenience, the information is arranged in
alphabetical order.

AGATE

Agate is a translucent or opaque quartz that has
two forms. It occurs either as a mass of clouded

color and pattern or as bands of distinct color. Most agate is gray in its natural state; the spectacular color of polished slabs in rock shops usually is artificial.

Light agate shot through with dark, feathery designs is known as *moss agate* because the tiny patterns appear to be fossilized moss. It isn't. It's a crystallization of *pyrolusite,* a form of manganese, that has leaked into cracks in the stone.

Onyx is banded quartz, usually black and white, although it sometimes occurs in red and white bands called *carnelian onyx* and brown and white bands called *sardonyx.* Since most quartz is around 7 on the Mohs scale, onyx is ideal for carving durable *cameos,* raised reliefs, or *intaglios,* recessed reliefs. Any stone that occurs in layers can be carved in this fashion, but all cameos are not onyx. If the cameo's colors are cream and caramel, for example, it's likely to have been carved from a seashell rather than onyx. *Shell cameos* are lovely in their own right, but not nearly as durable as onyx.

Mexican onyx, also called *cave onyx,* isn't onyx at all but a soft, banded marble that ranks about 3 on the Mohs scale. This "onyx" is the one frequently found in gift and curio shops in the form of bangles, goblets, elephants, donkeys, and bookends against which small men wearing sombreros lean in order to take their siestas.

Dull gray onyx can be artificially colored to resemble the more valuable black variety by boiling it in a sugar solution, then dipping it into sulphuric acid, which carbonizes the absorbed sugar, turning it black. The safest protection against this sort of thing is to buy your onyx from a reputable jeweler who will back up the sale with written assurances that the gem has not been color-treated.

ALEXANDRITE

Alexandrite is a chameleon among transparent gemstones, changing its color depending on the light source and the angle at which one views it. By daylight it has a predominantly green cast; by incandescent light it ranges from reddish orange to reddish purple. Genuine stones of good quality are quite costly, and so are synthetics, known as *alexandrine*.

Named for Alexander II, a 19th-century Russian czar, the stone is relatively rare. The best specimens come from Russia and Sri Lanka, with examples of lower quality being mined in Madagascar.

Alexandrite is a chrysoberyl, a gem family that ranks 8.5 on the Mohs scale, just below rubies and sapphires. It is therefore relatively hard.

AMETHYST

Amethysts are transparent, purplish varieties of quartz. They rarely cost more than a few hundred dollars, although amethysts in antique settings or combined with other gemstones can be more expensive. *Oriental amethysts* are actually purple corundum, a poorly colored ruby. Purple glass is a common substitute for amethyst.

BLOODSTONE

In spite of what you may have been told at the five and dime when you were a child, bloodstone is not a transparent red stone that looks like ruby. It's an opaque, dark green chalcedony flecked with bright red spots of jasper.

Bloodstone is usually cut either en cabochon or in flat ovals. It's also known as *heliotrope*.

CAIRNGORM

Cairngorm is a yellow to smoky-brown, transparent quartz that comes from the Cairngorm mountains in Scotland. If you have any kind of antique brooch, pin, or bracelet with thistles on it, the yellow stone is supposed to be cairngorm, although it may be yellow glass. Modern pieces probably substitute a smoky quartz, because the

93

Scotch supply is now virtually exhausted after centuries of mining.

CARNELIAN

There is very little true carnelian on the market; most of what passes for the real thing is pale chalcedony died an appropriate reddish-brown. Like the distinction between emeralds and beryl, the line dividing carnelian from sard is mainly one of perception. When the colors are a definite red and a definite brown, it's easy to make the distinction, but as they approach one another, the difference is mainly in the eye of the mineralogist or advertising copywriter.

CAT'S EYE

Cat's eye is not a gem but a phenomenon formally known as *chatoyancy,* a wavy, glowing band centered in a cabochon-cut gemstone. Chatoyancy occurs in a number of minerals when tiny mineral fibers such as asbestos or rutile are lined up parallel to one another so that they give off multiple reflections of the same ray of light. Chatoyancy is related to asterism, which produces the "star" of star sapphires and the *shiller,* or glow, of moonstones.

Oriental, or *precious, cat's eye* is the most valuable. It's a yellow to greenish chrysoberyl that casts a glowing band of purplish light. Precious cat's eye is also known as *cymophane*.

Occidental cat's eye is a greenish to grayish green quartz; in spite of its name, it too comes from the Far East. *Corundum cat's eye* is a star ruby or sapphire flawed to the point where the star is reduced to a single, glowing zone. Chatoyancy also occurs in *tourmaline*.

Tiger's eye, or *African cat's eye,* is either rich yellow and brown *crocidolite* or banded quartz. *Hawk's eye* is a blue-gray or green version of either crocidolite or quartz.

CHRYSOPRASE

A translucent, apple-green quartz, chrysoprase is one of the loveliest of the chalcedonies. Unfortunately, it's also fragile, and prolonged exposure to heat or sunlight will cause it to fade. Chrysoprase is also known as *apple jade*.

CITRINE

Often sold under the name *topaz quartz,* citrine is a lemony- to brownish-yellow, very rare in nature. True yellow citrines command high prices. However, the stones are easily manufactured by subjecting crystalline quartz to heat treatment, so obtain a written guarantee if you're intent on getting the genuine article.

GARNET

Garnet refers to several related silica-based minerals rather than to a single variety. In addition to the familiar wine red, garnets range from pink through brown and black, including green, yellow, and colorless, the color differences due to the inclusion of different chemical elements. The darker colors often are cut as hollow cabochons to allow light to penetrate the stone.

Most garnets in antique costume jewelry, especially from the Victorian era, are *Bohemian garnets,* a dark wine-red variety of *pyrope* mined in Czechoslovakia (part of which was formerly the German state of Bohemia). Pyrope garnets from South Africa are called *Cape rubies.* Violet red *almandine garnets,* also called *Adelaide rubies,* are found in Brazil, Sri Lanka, and India. Although few of these terms are used by contemporary jewelers, they still survive in the antique business and in popular usage.

Gooseberry garnets, also called *grossularite* or *hessonite garnets,* are light green, pink, gray, or brown. *Topazolite garnets* are yellowish, *melanites* are black, *demantoid* garnets are apple green to emerald green, the greener the better, with good fire and brilliant luster.

HEMATITE

Hematite is a brilliant opaque steel-gray to black crystal easily carved into cameos, intaglios, and shimmering beads. It's basically a form of iron ore.

JADE

Unlike the garnets, which are closely related to one another, the jades arc two very distinct translucent minerals: *nephrite,* composed of calcium, magnesium, and iron, and *jadeite,* composed of sodium, silicon, and aluminum.

In ancient times, jade was believed to be useful for curing kidney disorders. The Spaniards who discovered jadeite in Mexico named it *piedra de ijada,* or "stone of the loins"; the term was soon corrupted to "jade." When the chemical differences between the New World jade and Oriental jade were discovered, the latter was named nephrite, from a German word meaning "kidney mineral."

Nephrite is the stuff of the ancient Orient. Although it is not particularly scratch resistant, ranking 5.5 to 6.5 on the Mohs scale, its crystals are fibrous and matted together, so that nephrite is a tough gemstone and can be carved into delicate forms that are not nearly as fragile as they appear.

The classic nephrite color is emerald to spinach green, but it also occurs in brown, yellow, gray, black, blue, and a near-white that has the distressing name of muttonfat jade.

Jadeite, first discovered by Spanish explorers on a foray into Mexico, is harder than nephrite (6.5 to 7 on the Mohs scale), but its well-defined crystals are more inclined to shatter. It's mined chiefly in Burma and Mexico, although China has been importing it since the 1700s.

Colors of jadeite include the brilliant green known as imperial jade, as well as pure white, muttonfat, reddish brown, yellow brown, violet to magenta, and blue green.

Both nephrite and jadeite have a host of imitations. *Bowenite,* also called *new jade,* is a variety of serpentine that ranks 6 on the Mohs scale; only a laboratory test can distinguish the difference between bowenite and nephrite or jadeite. Other imitations are softer, however, and may yield their secrets to a knife test in an inconspicuous place. Imitators include *Mexican onyx,* a soft green-stained marble; agate, garnets, glass, soapstone, quartzite (a form of sandstone), californite, prehnite, saussurite, and zoisite.

Oregon jade is green jasper (see below), and *apple jade* is chrysoprase.

JASPER

Jasper is an opaque quartz that can be red, brown, green, or yellow. Its natural color often is intensified by dye. Jasper frequently appears in jewelry that evokes the American west.

LAPIS LAZULI

The most valuable specimens of this soft, deep blue, opaque mineral are uniform in color, although lapis with golden flecks of iron pyrite (fool's gold) and occasionally of real gold has become the standard in most people's minds. At 5.5 to 6 on the Mohs scale, lapis is more suited to beads and brooches than to rings or bangles. It sometimes has white streaks or blotches of calcite, which lower its value.

MALACHITE

Malachite is another soft (3.5 to 4 Mohs) mineral, an opaque, light-green copper ore marbled with dark, or dark green marbled with light, depending on your point of view. It often is used for inlay work, desk and dressing table appointments, flat brooches, and round beads.

MOONSTONE

Precious moonstone is translucent feldspar, either gray or bluish gray, that shimmers when the stone is turned in the light. The effect is caused by alternating layers of feldspar, each of which treats light a bit differently so that the eye perceives the reflections as being out of sync. The effect is known as *shiller* or *adularescence.*

Precious moonstone also is called *oriental moonstone.* Other translucent minerals that pass for moonstone include milky chalcedony or corundum too clouded with rutile to make a distinct star or cat's eye.

Moonstone ranks 6 on the Mohs scale.

OBSIDIAN

Obsidian is known to rockhounds as *Apache tear* and, with opal, is one of the few minerals to lack a crystalline structure. A natural glass formed in volcanic eruptions, it is black to gray in color, and, at 5 to 5.5 on the Mohs scale, easily carved into various shapes.

As a gemstone, it has little commercial value outside of souvenir shops.

PERIDOT

A transparent variety of the mineral olivine, peridot is a distinctive yellow-green gem, sometimes described as bottle green because of its similarity to the color of Coca-Cola bottles used earlier in this century. Also called *evening emerald,* peridot has little fire but a lovely, glossy appearance. It ranks 6.5 to 7 on the Mohs scale.

PRASE

Apple green chalcedony. See chrysoprase.

QUARTZ

Among the most desirable transparent quartzes are *rose quartz,* a deep pink stone that sometimes shows asterism, and *rock crystal,* a clear, glassy variety. Rock crystal is clear quartz from the Rhine valley in Germany and Austria, the original "Rhine stone." The term was quite respectable before it was cheapened by foil-backed glass imitations.

Smoky quartz is light to deep brown quartz, including cairngorm. It's also known as *smoky topaz* or *topaz quartz.*

SPINEL

A lovely gem in its own right, spinel suffers from the inevitable comparison to ruby. Often called *mother of ruby,* spinel is a brilliant, hard gemstone ranking just below corundum on the hardness scale. It usually is flawless, and is relatively abundant in stones smaller than ten carats, although scarcer in larger stones.

Ruby spinel is red, *balas ruby* or *balas spinel* is rose-colored, *rubicelle* tends toward orange, and *almandine spinel* is violet. Translucent or opaque varieties can be green, brown, or yellow-brown as well.

TOPAZ

True topaz ranks 8 on the Mohs scale, but cleaves easily and is therefore relatively fragile. A rich sherry color is the most prized, although natural pink and reddish purple topazes are sought after as well. Most topaz, however, is colorless, and bears a superficial resemblance to diamond when brilliant cut.

Heat treatment is frequent, changing yellow topaz into pink or blue stones.

True topaz is called *precious topaz* to distinguish it from various brownish quartzes, such as citrine, cairngorm, and the so-called smoky topaz.

TOURMALINE

This little-known yet readily available transparent gemstone comes in a number of colors, some crystals combining two or three colors in bands across the width of the stone. Tourmaline also can be *dichroic,* which means that the shade changes as the gem is rotated, and some display chatoyancy. Red or pink tourmaline is the most valuable, and is called *rubellite.* Green tourmaline also is called *Brazil emerald;* blue, *indicolite;* brown, *dravite;* black, *schorl.* Colorless tourmaline is known as *achorite.*

Tourmaline is both tough and scratch-resistant, ranking 7 to 7.5 on the Mohs scale.

ZIRCON

Zircon is under the same cloud as spinel, a lovely gem in its own right but considerably more common than the more precious gem it resembles, which in this case is diamond. Zircon has even more fire than diamond, and occurs naturally in a rainbow of shades, with blue being the most preferred. Heat treatment produces both colorless and blue stones from off-colored specimens.

Most zircon today is found in antique pieces, having been replaced by synthetics such as *cubic zirconia*.

10

Making the Purchase

Whether you're interested in brand-new jewelry, good second-hand pieces (the trade euphemism for the latter is *estate jewelry*), or antique and other specialty items, you can do several things to increase your chances of acquiring something worth owning.

The first, of course, is to become familiar with the characteristics of the gemstones and precious metals, which is what you have been doing throughout this book.

The second is to select a jeweler or a dealer with as much care as you can give to the project. Guidelines to help you decide to whom to give your business are included in this chapter, which concentrates on buying from traditional retail outlets. Antique jewelry, American Indian jewelry, estate jewelry, and other specialized purchases are covered in the following chapter.

Shop around, and take your time when you decide to buy something. Gem prices can vary by thousands of dollars from year to year, depending on the supply, which fluctuates wildly depending on the strength of the dollar and the political stability of the countries where most of the gems are found.

Knowing what questions to ask and what documentation to get in writing also helps insure that your purchase matches your expectations. Suggestions in this area also are included in this chapter and the next.

Finally, you will help yourself a great deal if you acquire a jeweler's loupe, which is a small magnifying apparatus similar to the ones jewelers used to wear, monocle-style, in one eye. You won't need one that specialized unless you decide to learn to repair your own pieces and need two free hands; a small hand-held loupe of 10 power magnification (written as 10X on the device) is sufficient for examining a piece at close range. This is particularly important when considering the purchase of antique and estate pieces, which must be checked closely for signs of wear, damage to the stones, and clues to the composition of the metal in which the stones are set.

To use a loupe, hold it within an inch of your eye and move the gemstone or piece of jewelry up to the loupe. You may have to practice a few times in order to overcome the temptation to use it as if you were holding a magnifying glass.

Loupes are available in some hobby shops and through most scientific supply firms, rock shops and lapidaries, and all jewelers' supply houses. Check the Yellow Pages and do some advance telephoning first. If you live in an area where the phone company has seen fit to separate the business-to-business Yellow Pages from the consumer directory, you may have to consult the business version for jewelers' and science supply firms. Usually, you can obtain a copy of the business pages by calling your phone company.

KINDS OF RETAIL OUTLETS

Unless you have a close relative in the wholesale gem business, you probably will have to rely on a retail jeweler for your pearls and peridots. Just as all diamonds are not created equal, neither are jewelry stores, as a walk through any suburban shopping mall will show you. Not counting the earring boutiques, you are likely to encounter one or several of the following, depending on the size of the mall:

- A store specializing exclusively in diamond engagement rings and matching wedding bands.

- A store concentrating on the above, which also carries a selection of flatware (knives, forks, and spoons in sterling and silver plate), holloware (tea services, platters, silver salt and pepper snakers, etc.), crystal, giftware of silver plate and porcelain, including favors suitable for engraving for the wedding party, gilt clocks in glass domes, and watches. These stores can be thought of as one-stop wedding accessory centers.

- A department store with a fine jewelry counter or department.

- A full-service jewelry store aimed at middle-income customers, offering a full range of jewelry in standard *findings* (ring, brooch, necklace, bracelet, and pendant mountings), including a selection of natural and synthetic colored stones of medium price and quality.

- A store aimed at high-income customers that concentrates on fine jewelry and top-of-the-line watches.

It is a given that one stays away from stores that use their windows to advertise 50 percent-off sales in letters a foot high or that display prices that can be read from the other side of the street. Stores of this sort are geared to the truly unsophisticated customer, with gems of corresponding quality. It is best to confine your shopping to a carriage-trade store, where the price is not significantly greater considering the service one is likely to get, the fine jewelry department of an upscale department store, or a reputable full-service store where you have found a salesperson who is both knowledgeable and trustworthy.

Although the latter may not have as extensive or as top-grade a selection on hand as a more exclusive retailer, any reputable jeweler can obtain additional selections for you to consider, in any price range. The carriage-trade stores will offer this to you automatically ("If none of these sapphires are what you're looking for, we can have another selection for madam to choose from tomorrow"); in the less exclusive stores, you may have to ask.

Generally speaking, you are safe with a store or a jeweler that is a member of the American Gem Society, a professional association of fine jewelers whose members pledge to abide by a strict code of ethics. AGS members often display the society's emblem in their advertisements and Yellow Pages listings. If you can't locate any in your immediate area, write or call the American Gem Society, 5901 West Third Street, Los Angeles, CA 90036 [(213) 936-4367] and ask for the names of members in your area.

THE STORE ITSELF

Having located a suitable outlet, take a moment to assure yourself that the store's interior is as promising as its public face. Are the display cases conveniently arranged? Is the merchandise displayed neatly? Is there seating so that you can examine a piece in comfort?

Pay special attention to the lighting above the counters. If the bulbs are colored, especially blue, find another store with which to do business. Any gemstone will look lovely in blue light, particularly yellowish diamonds. Most stores will have a row of recessed lights above the counter to show off gemstones and jewelry metal to their very best advantage, but the better stores also will have a counter fixture with a fluorescent bulb color-balanced to provide light comparable to natural daylight. This is where you want to examine any item you're serious about purchasing. Taking a ring to a window or stepping outside with the jeweler is a poor substitute, and impossible in an enclosed mall. If a store does not have such a fixture, eliminate the store from your consideration.

SALESPEOPLE

In any store, the most important factor is the training and attitude of the staff. Ideally, all the salespeople who deal with diamonds, colored stones, or jewelry repair will have the appropriate certification either from the Gemological Institute of America (GIA), the industry's education, research, and testing arm, or the American Gem Society. Staff with these credentials can be presumed to be knowledgeable about their particular field.

Gemologists have GIA certification in gemstone identification as well as in diamonds and colored stones, and therefore are proficient in all aspects of fine gemstones. AGS certification includes Registered Jeweler, Certified Gemologist, and Certified Gemologist Appraiser, each

with rigorous education and testing require-
ments for annual renewal of certification.

Beyond suitable credentials, the staff's attitude is an important consideration. There is no
excuse for snootiness or fast talk in a good jewelry store. If you are not greeted with respect,
excuse yourself and leave the premises. A good
salesperson should treat you as if you are interested in, and well able to afford, a matched
strand of natural pearls or a bracelet of D-flaw-
less diamonds, and should explain fully any
terms you don't understand and disclose any
chemical or other special treatment to which the
gemstone you're interested in has been subjected.

A good way to check a salesperson's trust-
worthiness is to inquire about a gemstone
you're already well versed in, and to ask your
questions without tipping your hand. For example, if you are interested in star sapphires, first
ask the salesperson to see a selection of rings. If
the asterism is too well defined, you can suspect
that the ones before you are synthetics; if less
defined, you believe them to be natural stones.
Don't try to impress the clerk with your knowledge, however; take your time and see where he
or she will lead you. Ask for some information
about them ("What can you tell me about star
sapphires?"). If you receive a reasonable explanation of the phenomenon of asterism, but still

no hint that the stones in front of you are natural or synthetic, either the clerk does not know there is a difference or has prejudged the amount you are willing to spend. Now is the time to press a bit further by remarking that it's amazing to see so many perfectly formed stars (if they're synthetic) or that these are fuzzier than you expected—why is that?

On the other hand, if you are presented with a mixed selection, you have an opportunity to ask about the difference between the clearly defined stars and the fuzzier ones.

Once you have found a salesperson both competent and trustworthy, throw coyness out the window and be straightforward about what you want to see—for example, a natural citrine or a one-carat, brilliant-cut diamond solitaire, no lower in quality than F VVS_2.

EXAMINING THE ITEM

When you have narrowed your selection to items of the style and color you desire, ask to see each piece under natural light. Now is the time to extract your loupe from pocket or purse. Look carefully at the back of the piece to check for scratches or evidence of poor workmanship, such as burrs of metal or places where the polishing is rough. Look for stampings that indicate the quality of the metal used, and ask about any you do not understand.

Next look carefully at how the gemstones are mounted, checking to see if the setting holds the stone securely.

Finally, examine the gemstones from all angles. On faceted stones, look carefully at how the facets are cut; if your relatively untrained eye sees anything carelessly cut or polished, eliminate the item from your consideration or, if you're absolutely in love with the setting, ask about having the offending stone replaced with one of better quality. Pay attention, too, to the color of the stone and whether it displays the characteristics of a good specimen of that mineral. Look at the stone from the side as well as from the top; this is especially important for cabochon stones in order to detect doublets or triplets.

This is the time to ask whether the stone has received any color treatment, and if so, how permanent it is. It's also a good idea to ask whether any comparable stones are available that have not been color treated; a natural stone may be entirely out of your price range but then again, it may not be. It doesn't cost anything to ask.

In the better stores, you often will be offered the opportunity of selecting stones and mountings separately. This gives you the opportunity of customizing your jewelry at little or no extra cost. (Jewelry produced in this manner should not be confused with the one-of-a-kind pieces custom-made by a goldsmith, however; the latter are handmade items while the former use mass-produced findings.) Customizing is a way to individualize your jewelry, comparable to ordering a car from the factory to your specifications rather than buying one right from the showroom floor. (The wait for delivery, however, is considerably shorter!) For example, if you desire garnet earstuds to match an antique ring, you can specify that they be set in a six-prong mount rather than the standard four-prong, thus adding a subtle touch of luxury.

HOW THE RECEIPT SHOULD READ

A salesperson should be willing to back up in writing any statement he or she makes about a particular piece of jewelry. This includes providing you with a written receipt detailing not only the date and price of the purchase, but also:

- An overall description of the piece (round 2-inch brooch, 24-inch graduated pearl necklace, etc.)

- Composition of metals used in the setting or clasp

- Size of the gemstones, with carats in millimeters or grains as appropriate

- Shape of the gemstones (brilliant cut, flat oval, cabochon, baguette, etc.)

- Minerals involved, and whether they are natural or synthetic, treated or untreated

- Color of the gemstones, with appropriate distinctions between color grades for gems such as diamond

- Clarity of the stones where appropriate

Obviously, some of this information will not be applicable for the less valuable stones.

Such a receipt might read "one-carat diamond solitaire in white gold Tiffany setting, G color VS_1," or "one 18-inch double-oval link neckchain in 14K gold, spring ring clasp."

When buying any gem costing more than a few hundred dollars, especially in diamonds, rubies, sapphires, emeralds, and aquamarines, ask the jeweler to have the gem's authenticity verified in a GIA lab and to provide you with a GIA report to that effect. There will be a fee for this service, and it will delay your purchase somewhat, but the precaution is well worth taking because you will be living with a major purchase for a long time. If the gem does not receive a positive GIA report, a reputable jeweler will refund your money. If you absolutely must wear the piece to a White House reception this weekend, you may have to arrange for a GIA lab report at a later date. Be sure to clear this with your jeweler, because unless you are a known customer, he or she may be reluctant to stand by a stone that has left the store and thus been subjected to the risk of damage or stone-switching.

11

Antique
and Other Specialty
Jewelry Purchases

In many ways, buying antique jewelry, American Indian jewelry, or other specialty items is identical to purchasing contemporary jewelry at a retail establishment. One should know one's dealer, pay close attention to the workmanship of the item, and go into the purchase knowing as much as possible about what one wants to buy.

But each specialty also has unique aspects as well. While the guidelines in this chapter are not meant to be a comprehensive examination of each category, following them will help you avoid major mistakes in your purchases.

ANTIQUE JEWELRY

What makes a piece of jewelry an antique? Having survived 100 years is the answer the U.S. Customs Service gives in exempting pieces of that age from import fees if they have the proper papers. In popular usage, however, antique jewelry is anything acquired two or three generations ago, with Art Deco jewelry of the 1920s and 1930s on the borderline between antique and vintage. Most of what is readily available in this country is Civil War era, late Victorian, and turn-of-the-century, although older pieces are more abundant on the East Coast and in parts of the South that have been settled since colonial times.

Materials Used

Until the Industrial Revolution, jewelry was for the most part an indulgence of the well-to-do. With the advent of industrial techniques, which hit this country in the late 1840s and early 1850s, mass-produced jewelry became available to average folk. While not crafted of precious metals and precious stones, this costume jewelry of the 19th century can be quite valuable today. Some of it was quite lovely, and some of it, while not particularly attractive to the modern eye, is valuable not because of its looks but because of the material from which it is made. Because it was inexpensive, it did not receive the same care as a fine gem in a precious metal setting. When the owner tired of it, it was more likely to be discarded or given to the children to play with than to be put away for future generations. In addition, because the workmanship on an inexpensive piece often left much to be desired, it was less expensive to replace a brooch with a broken clasp than to have the clasp repaired. Consequently, such material is relatively scarce, and correspondingly expensive.

Materials in pieces of this sort include *gutta-percha,* a dark brown-to-black mixture of latex, resin, and sawdust that was molded into various shapes, particularly beads and brooches, around the time of the American Civil War. *Bog oak* is a dark oak dug up from the peat bogs of Ireland and carved, often with designs evoking the Auld Sod. *German silver,* also called *nickel silver,* is an alloy in the general proportions of 65% copper, 17% zinc, and 18% nickel, used in jewelry and cutlery as imitation silver.

Hair jewelry, either made from the hair of a loved one, usually deceased, or enclosing a lock of hair, was another form of jewelry unique to the Victorian era. Sometimes the piece was entirely woven of hair; other times hair and precious metals were combined.

Cut steel, an early form of steel, was often faceted to give sparkle to buckles and pins. All faceted metal is not necessarily cut steel, however; nickel silver was frequently molded into faceted shapes. The difference is that cut steel facets have sharp edges while the edges of molded facets are soft. In addition, the molded pieces are riveted to a backing, while cut steel is usually in one piece.

At one point in the mid-19th century, *aluminum* was quite the rage for jewelry, being at that time a rare and costly metal. The bottom fell out of the market, however, when the process for producing aluminum in commercial quantities was developed in the late 1880s.

With the exception of these non-precious materials, used mainly in the 19th century, and platinum, which came into its own in this century, better antique jewelry was made with the same gemstones and precious metals as contemporary pieces. The difference is in how the jewelry was worn and in the styles it took. Elaborate hatpins, jeweled shoe and hat ornaments, watch fobs, and massive *stomachers* (brooches suited to the ample girth of the fashionable matron of the 1880s) have few counterparts today. On the other hand, the rings, stickpins, chains, and smaller brooches of by-gone eras are still completely usable today.

How to Become a Knowledgeable Buyer

Antique jewelry is a complex field, one which could easily fill a book of its own. Unfortunately, few such books have been written, except those concentrating on truly ancient pieces and the gifts of royalty to one another, and most of those that have been published are now out of print. The main branch of a major public library may be your only resource for written reference material; a good place to begin is with a book entitled *Antique Jewelry: A Practical and Passionate Guide,* by Rose Leiman Goldenberg (1976, Crown Publishers), which provides a good general introduction to the subject. Further study can be pursued in more general books on metalwork and jewelry that include sections on late 18th to early 20th century jewelry.

A step to take concurrently with your research is to visit antique shows. You will soon discover that there are dealers who specialize in antique jewelry, as well as dealers who have only a tray or two of mixed pieces among the painted china and pressed glass. For now, give the specialists your attention, because they're the ones most likely to have both the correct answers to your questions and the better quality goods.

Some retail jewelers also have a showcase of antique jewelry, although most of what they will display will be estate pieces of fairly recent vintage.

As with any jewelry purchase, pay attention to how the goods are displayed and whether they appear to be both in good condition and of high quality. In general, a dealer whose display cases are clean and who has arranged good examples of various items in an attractive manner is to be preferred to one who displays tray upon tray of mediocre rings or inferior brooches. Just because something is old does not give it automatic value.

Choosing a Dealer

Until you gain experience and confidence in your own judgment, it's safest to confine your purchases to a dealer or dealers in whom you have confidence. Unlike retail sales, there are usually no standards antique jewelry dealers must meet other than routine municipal licensing for resale, and the dealer who has taken the trouble to pursue the GIA course of studies is rare indeed. However, a dealer who belongs to a state or national association of antique dealers may have to meet higher standards than one who does not, and a dealer exhibiting at an exclusive show at which an admission is charged is likely to have a selection that is higher in quality overall than a dealer who is exhibiting at a free-to-the-public show in a shopping mall.

A reputable dealer will provide you with a detailed receipt that describes your purchase along the lines discussed in the previous chapter, with the addition of the approximate age of the piece, which usually can be determined from its style. Early brooches, for instance, have a simple C-clasp made of bent wire; the more secure safety catch did not come into widespread use until after 1900.

How to Inspect Antique Jewelry

Regardless of your confidence in the dealer, be certain to inspect each piece thoroughly and carefully before you buy. Using your loupe, check each gemstone for scratches, cracks, and chipped facets. Look carefully for signs of wear on metal, especially rings. If the piece is gold-plated, some of the base metal may show through. If the piece shows no visible signs of wear at all, ask the jeweler why it doesn't; perhaps it has been repolished, which should lower its value in your eyes if you are after genuine antiques, or perhaps it is a reproduction.

Check also for signs of repair, including gray

solder marks on the undersides of rings or brooches. Resolve to buy only the best of the best, but do not be put off by subtle signs of wear, only major flaws. After all, a beautiful old necklace that has been loved is bound to show some signs of its past life.

AMERICAN INDIAN JEWELRY

Silver jewelry set with turquoise is instantly recognizable as Native American jewelry of the Southwest tribes. Like all other jewelry, however, the quality of such pieces varies greatly, depending on the skill of the artisan and the materials used. Moreover, all jewelry made in the Indian style is not necessarily handmade, made by Native Americans, or even "made in the U.S.A."

Materials Used

Virtually all new pieces use sterling silver. *Coin silver* pieces, made from melted United States or Mexican currency, have not been legally made since anti-melting laws were passed in the 1890s. Genuine coin silver jewelry, therefore, is nearly always an antique by any definition and costs a mint. The alloy is slightly less pure than sterling, and has a yellowish cast if the jewelry is made from melted United States money, due to the high copper content of the alloy. Coin silver from Mexican currency has less copper and more a bluish cast.

Pawn silver refers not to an alloy but to how the jewelry was acquired by a dealer. Half a century ago, it was common for tribal members to pawn their jewelry to get their families through the lean times before the harvest, and to redeem the pieces when money was again available. When the pieces were sold by the pawnbroker before they could be redeemed, the dealers who bought them called them pawn silver to play on the heartstrings of their customers.

Turquoise is the gemstone most frequently associated with jewelry of the Southwest tribes, although jasper and mother-of-pearl are also common. As you remember from the section on turquoise earlier in the book, there is precious little precious turquoise left in the world—turquoise of a natural deep sky-blue that is strong enough to resist fading and cracking without special treatment. The turquoise in all but the finest authentic Indian pieces today is treated or stabilized turquoise.

However, all other things being equal, the presence of stabilized turquoise in an otherwise authentic piece is not necessarily a liability. Further, authentic jewelry traditionally has contained stone that looks like turquoise, but isn't.

Often this is not an intent to deceive on the part of the artisan, but a concern for effect that overrides chemistry. Such substitutes include malachite, lapis, green chalcedony, agate, and quartz—occasionally even plastic. The important thing in this regard is whether the artisan and/or dealer is open about the substitutions. If you are intent on assembling a collection of the finest silver and turquoise available, you'll want to pass up pieces that include substitutes. If you're more interested in authentic tribal pieces than in authentic turquoise, you may have no objection to the substitution as long as you know what you're buying.

Forms of Tribal Jewelry

Although some tribal artisans now are working in contemporary forms using traditional materials, the bulk of the serious work is in the classical designs associated with each tribe.

Navajo work tends to emphasize heavy silver forms and symmetrical designs, using gemstones only as complements to the metal.

Zuni work is more delicate and naturalistic in style, using more and smaller stones for inlay, mosaic work, and channel work, the latter being a sort of cloisonné using flat gemstones rather than enamel. Other Zuni motifs are clusters of smaller stones around a central one; row upon row of closely set cabochons of the same size; and needlepoint, which is row work with small, narrow, pointed ovals rather than rounded stones.

A favored *Hopi* technique involves joining together two layers of metal and then cutting designs through the top layer to expose the bottom layer. The lower layer is then darkened by oxidation, and the top layer is polished. The contrast produces a striking three-dimensional design, usually geometrical. Hopi work seldom uses gemstones.

Work of the *Santo Domingo* is primarily beadwork in tubular silver and stabilized turquoise. The finest examples use only smooth handmade beads of uniform size that ripple like ropes of blue water and liquid silver.

Tribal jewelry includes bangles, earrings, brooches, belt buckles, rings, and necklaces. *Conchas,* or *conch belts,* are oval silver pieces, with or without gemstones, that are strung together with leather thongs. A *squash blossom necklace* is a necklace of hollow silver beads and silver flower forms, from which hangs a crescent-shaped pendant. Turquoise usually is involved.

Stay away from pieces whose only claim to authenticity is that they are *reservation made* or *Indian made.* Chances are they are machine made, and although the machine may very well have been on a reservation, or operated by a full-blooded Native American, or both, the jewelry is still a factory product, not a piece hand-crafted by a skilled artisan. Another term that should raise an eyebrow is *hand-finished;* it means that a mass-produced piece has been polished by hand, or that the stones were set in by hand.

How to Find a Reputable Dealer

If you live in the Southwest or California, you'll have more access to tribal jewelry than someone in Minneapolis or Cincinnati, but that doesn't mean you'll do better. It all depends on the dealer with whom you do business. As with all fine jewelry purchases, it's important to choose an established dealer with an impeccable reputation, and then to seek an independent appraisal for any major purchase.

This means avoiding auctions unless they're conducted by an established house that makes a printed catalogue available in advance, avoiding half-price and bargain sales from carts on city sidewalks, avoiding jewelry sold from hotel rooms and in motel gift shops, at state fairs, and in Tupperware-style house parties.

Whether buying in the shops of Albuquerque or the canyons of Manhattan, look for a dealer who belongs to the Indian Arts and Crafts Association. Such a dealer will display the IACA emblem somewhere in the shop, and while membership is no guarantee that the shop carries top-of-the-line merchandise, IACA members are obliged to voluntarily inform customers whether a piece is authentic and whether the gemstone is natural, treated, stabilized, or synthetic.

A reputable dealer also will provide a written receipt that includes every claim he or she has made about the piece, including price, date of purchase, a detailed description, materials used, tribal origin, name of the artisan who made it, and whether it is hand- or machine-crafted.

MUSEUM REPRODUCTIONS

Lovely jewelry is sometimes available in the gift shops and through the catalogues of major museums. Most reproductions are vermeil or plate, but some jewelry is 14K or 18K gold and, in the less flamboyant designs, a fine addition to any collection. Prices are comparable to contemporary jewelry when one considers that the pieces are produced in much smaller quantities.

Although in many cases you will be buying the merchandise on the strength of the photograph and description in the catalogue, rather than after a close first-hand examination, you are protected both by the museum's reputation and its return policy. To avoid disappointment, remember that authentic reproduction jewelry usually will not be as sharply defined as contemporary jewelry; for instance, faceting gemstones is a fairly recent development. From ancient times to the early Renaissance, gemstones were cut to preserve their size, not to capitalize on how they handled light. If there is faceting, it is likely to be uneven, and the piece may lack complete symmetry. After all, the originals from which the reproductions are made often have survived fire and war, and may bear the marks of their turbulent life.

All reproductions are discreetly marked as such; this is to prevent people less ethical than you from reselling them as authentic.

When considering the purchase of museum reproductions, don't get carried away to the point of violating your personal style. Cher can get away with bangle earrings in the form of stylized Abyssinian lions, but if your taste runs to tailored suits and sedate evening dress, you might get more steady use out of a chaste little Merovingian garnet ring.

CUSTOM-MADE JEWELRY

Independent goldsmiths, who often exhibit at the better craft fairs, are a good source for distinctive, one-of-a-kind pieces. You usually can either buy directly from the goldsmith's stock or work with the artisan to create a piece to your specifications.

When buying custom-made jewelry, you should follow much the same procedure you would in any retail store. Take your loupe along, and examine everything carefully, asking questions about anything you don't understand, questions ranging from why the stone is mounted in such and such a fashion to why the surface has more texture on one side than on the other. Because custom goldsmiths are artists as well as jewelers, they are more willing to experiment with size, texture, and combinations of materials than jewelers who must cater to a more diverse, less adventuresome customer base. Therefore, expect the unusual, but don't be shy about asking questions about it.

Your best procedure in buying custom-made jewelry is to scout the craft fairs for a season, talk to the artisans about their work, and acquire the business cards of those whose work appeals to you. Then call to make appointments to see their collections privately, when you will not be forced to make your decisions in the middle of a crowd.

It's best to make major purchases only from artists and craftspeople who have been in business for several years. Most college art majors go through a phase during which they're convinced they want to work exclusively in jewelry design; you will, of course, purchase some inexpensive pieces from them to encourage their talent, but save your major purchases for those who have persevered in their dream despite the realities of the business world.

COSTUME JEWELRY

Costume jewelry, also called *fashion jewelry,* is not necessarily either tacky or inexpensive, although much of it assuredly is. For the purposes of definition, consider costume jewelry to be anything not made with precious gems, precious metals, or both. It can be as expensive as several hundred dollars for very good synthetic (or "faux") gemstones set to look like the real thing, or as inexpensive as $5.95 for a pair of white enamel earrings to wear with a sundress.

Materials include plastic, wood, aluminum, stainless steel (the Scandinavians are especially good at producing striking designs in stainless steel), vermeil, gold-tone metal, enamels, cloisonné, papier-mâché, straw . . . the list is limited only by what's in fashion this year.

And passing fashion is exactly where costume jewelry comes into its own. It's foolish to pay hundreds or thousands of dollars for something that will look dated in five years at the most, but it makes very good sense to spend $5 or $25 on jewelry that enhances a trendy outfit. Because the workmanship and materials that go into costume jewelry aren't of the quality of fine jewelry, the jewelry won't last as long—but it doesn't have to.

Costume jewelry also has its place in casual wear. Although discreet pearl earrings are supposed to be able to complement any outfit, sometimes small wooden or ceramic earrings just feel more appropriate with jeans and a turtleneck.

The rules for buying costume jewelry are similar to those for buying more expensive jewelry. Buy the best you can afford and inspect each piece carefully for surface flaws, although you may forego the use of your loupe. Check how firmly the gemstones are set; they shouldn't wiggle under the pressure of your finger. Look for smears of enamel on the metal. Work the clasps to be sure that they work and are secure. When buying necklaces of beads, those strung with individual knots between each bead are preferable to those strung all in a line; if the necklace should break, an individually knotted string will lose, at the most, one or two beads. Earring clasps, whether post-and-nut for pierced ears or clips for intact lobes, should be firm yet easy to operate.

12

Care, Cleaning,
and Culling
Your Collection

The check you hand to your jeweler or mail to your credit card company isn't the last money you'll be spending in this area of your life. Dramatic major pieces often are enhanced by less elaborate secondary pieces, such as small earrings that complement a major pin or necklace.

Other costs you will incur over the years include annual insurance premiums, reappraisals, and routine maintenance for some items, such as stones that need to be replaced or rings that need to be stretched a half size. As your collection increases, you may decide to acquire a household safe or bank safe-deposit box for your more valuable pieces.

You also will spend a small amount of time and an insignificant amount of money on jewelry care and maintenance, particularly on diamonds and the fragile gems. Although this is a chore that can be measured in seconds rather than hours over the course of the year, it is nevertheless important in order to preserve the quality of your jewelry.

This chapter discusses all of these topics. In addition, it discusses options for disposing of seldom-worn or outmoded pieces.

ASSEMBLING A WARDROBE OF FINE JEWELRY

Because jewelry is very much a matter of personal taste, it's difficult to give advice about what a woman should or need not own. Some people, for instance, can't abide bracelets. Others are comfortable only with an armload of bangles. Some prefer costume jewelry for the office and save the truly luxurious pieces for purely social occasions. Some can mix colored stones and different metals to good effect; others look merely gaudy when they try the same thing.

Probably the best advice for assembling a collection of fine jewelry is to follow your instincts. If your birthstone is topaz but your coloring cries aquamarine, either go with one of the pastel topazes or a lovely blue aquamarine. Birthstone designations (see Table 4 in the Appendix) are mainly marketing gimmicks anyway.

Presumably you have one or two pieces of fine jewelry already. Unless you are utterly dissatisfied with them, it makes sense to build on what you already have. For instance, if you have a gold wedding band, first add compatible earrings, a neckchain or more elaborate necklace, a bracelet, and a gold pin. If you add colored stones, keep them the same color.

Then vow solemnly never, ever, to wear everything at once. The idea behind having a *parure,* or matched set of jewelry, is to have versatility in your wardrobe, not to look like an advertisement for your particular specialty.

Similarly, if you have on hand a pearl necklace of good quality, set about finding some earrings that match the color of your beads exactly. Do not settle for earrings that are the slightest bit off-color if you intend to wear them with the necklace. You might not be able to tell the difference in the soft light of your home, but when you wear them to a job interview, be assured that someone important will notice.

HOW TO STORE FINE JEWELRY

The average velvet-lined jewelry box, with its multitude of compartments and possibly a tinkly music-box mechanism, can be a dangerous place to store fine jewelry. It is almost inevitable in such a situation that one piece will come in contact with another, and that is the last thing you want to happen. The softer gemstone or sofer metal of the two will be the loser. If the box receives a good jostling at the hands of a careless cleaning person or curious toddler, you will have the makings of a minor disaster: pearls tangled with brooches and charm bracelets and studded with inextricable earrings.

One way to avoid this scenario is to eliminate a central container and keep each piece in the box it came in. If you don't have the originals, find a jewelry supply house, where you can buy individual boxes complete with padded linings or boxes fitted with slotted inserts for holding a number of rings.

If you insist on using a jewelry box (and let's face it, most of us do), use one with as few separate compartments as possible and protect each piece by either wrapping it carefully in acid-free tissue paper or placing it in a bag of flannel, chamois, or plastic as appropriate to the gemstone involved (see below). The tissue paper is the sort dry cleaners use for preserving wedding gowns; beg a few sheets the next time you drop off your silk blouses. The bags are available from your jeweler, through jewelers' supply firms, and occasionally in upscale mail-order catalogues. The plastic ones also are obtainable in the bags-and-wraps section of your local supermarket. Look for the freezer-weight reclosable bags. For all but the delicate gems that need to breathe, these sandwich-sized bags may be the most sensible, if somewhat inelegant, mode of storage, because you can readily identify their contents.

Sterling silver can be stored in either plastic bags or flannel bags impregnated with an anti-tarnishing agent. But do not store silver set with gemstones in the latter, lest an adverse chemical reaction occur between the gemstone and the anti-tarnish agent. Use neither plastic nor impregnated flannel for pearls, opals, ivory, turquoise, amber, coral, or tortoise shell. These gems must be stored in a material that "breathes" so they will have access to air and humidity. If they must be stored in safes or safe-deposit boxes, be sure to remove them several times a year for a day or so to permit them access to fresh air.

Admittedly, storing your jewelry in this non-traditional fashion deprives you of the satisfaction of a readily viewable "treasury," but the sacrifice is small compared to the benefit of safeguarding your purchases from accidental damage.

In an ideal world, one then would store one's individually packaged jewels in one's household safe. Assuming you have yet to acquire this particular article, a dresser drawer may have to do for all but the most valuable pieces, with the latter spending most of their time in a bank safe-deposit box—inconvenient, but indisputably secure.

If you must take some or all of your jewelry with you when you travel, take the added precaution of wrapping each bag in tissue paper to further cushion it, and transport it either in your fiercely guarded purse or a carry-on bag that remains in your custody at all times.

INSURING YOUR JEWELRY

The moment you acquire jewelry worth a week's salary or more, call the agent who carries your homeowners' or tenants' policy and inquire about a *jewelry floater,* which is a policy that covers jewelry and other items that move about rather than stay in one place. Depending on your current coverage, a certain amount of jewelry may already be covered from theft, but it is wise to take no chances.

Furthermore, loss covered only by a homeowners' policy will be subject to deductions, while that covered by a floater usually will have no deductions, and a floater with an all-risk provision usually covers damage and accidental loss, in addition to theft. Accidental loss includes the loss of stones from a setting, as well as the loss of the entire piece of jewelry. Ask your insurance agent about all the options, and be sure you understand exactly what is and is not covered. Rates vary from company to company, but generally a floater policy is one of the more economical ones you can buy.

Unless the jewelry is a brand-new purchase for which you have a comprehensive sales slip, and often even then, your insurance company will require an appraisal for each piece you are insuring. There are several types of appraisals (see below), but the only one the insurance company is interested in is an appraisal to determine the jewelry's replacement cost. Since this cost generally increases with inflation, it is a good idea to have your jewelry reappraised at regular intervals, at least every five to seven years.

APPRAISALS

To have an *appraisal* done means taking a piece of jewelry to someone qualified to determine its replacement value, its market (resale) value, its gemological value, or all of the above. A GIA report, for instance, is an appraisal of a gemstone's authenticity, color, and grade, but not of monetary value.

An *insurance appraisal* is concerned with the cost of replacing a lost or stolen item, or of repairing a damaged one. Insurance appraisals are based on retail prices for gemstones and precious metals at the time of the appraisal.

A *market appraisal,* perhaps of your dear departed aunt's diamond earrings, is concerned with what the item can be sold for, which is far less than what it would cost to replace it. The market value depends on what someone is willing to pay for it, and unless your aunt was one of the last surviving Romanoffs, you are likely to realize only the wholesale value of the gemstones and precious metals.

Antique jewelry, of course, is another matter altogether, and an appraisal for resale purposes may very well bring more than the sum of the piece's individual components. It may take some searching to find a jeweler sufficiently knowledgeable to do a competent appraisal of antique jewelry, but it is worth the effort.

An *estate appraisal* for inheritance tax purposes is essentially the same as a resale appraisal, although it is devoutly to be wished that the appraiser in this instance will err on the side of conservatism.

It is a given that one does not request an appraisal from someone to whom one wishes to sell the jewelry, for it would not be in that person's best financial interests to make you a generous offer.

Appraisers who have either AGS certification or who belong to the International Society of Appraisers are your best bets for an accurate, above-board assessment of the worth of your jewelry. Appraisal fees vary from nothing at all at your friendly neighborhood jewelry store, to a flat fee that should be explained to you beforehand. Generally a jeweler will be willing to take a quick look at something to tell you if it is of sufficient value to be worth an appraisal. The fee is based on a jeweler's time, training, and the use of the instruments necessary to thoroughly examine the piece. At times, gemstones will have to be removed from their settings in order to be properly identified, but this is not the usual procedure.

Precious metals are generally identified by hallmarks, such as "14K" or "sterling," stamped somewhere on the underside of the piece or on the clasp. On antique pieces, however, you may have to settle for an educated guess, because most tests for determining the composition of metal beneath the surface are destructive of the metal in some way.

Gemstones are identified and evaluated by some or all of the following methods.

Refractive Index: This is the most important test for identification of a given gemstone. It measures the angle at which a gem bends a ray of light. It is usable for both transparent and opaque gemstones. The appraiser uses a *refractometer* to measure the angle of the light, and then consults a table. Each angle is very specific to each mineral species, so the gemstone can usually be readily identified. For instance, jadeite, nephrite, and serpentine, all of which can bear superficial resemblances to one another, have refractive indices that occur at distinctly different locations on the table.

High Magnification: This will check for growth lines, color zones, inclusions, and gas bubbles, which help determine whether a stone is natural or synthetic. High magnification will also reveal defects in the faceting or polishing that will lower the stone's value.

Absorption of Light: Many naturally colored stones absorb different portions of a light wave than do their treated or synthetic counterparts.

A jeweler using a *prism spectroscope* can distinguish between natural and irradiated diamonds, natural and synthetic corundum (rubies and sapphires), and other chemically identical gemstones.

Fluorescence: The reaction of a gem to ultraviolet light is sometimes helpful in distinguishing artificial stones from natural ones. This test, however, is a supplement to otherwise positive gem identification rather than one that absolutely identifies a gem; this is because some natural gems from one mine will *fluoresce* (glow), while other natural gems of the same species, mined elsewhere, will not.

X-ray: Used to determine whether a pearl is natural, cultured, or imitation when other means of identification don't work.

Other tests that are possible include a test for the gem's *specific gravity,* the weight of the gem compared either with the weight of an equal volume of water or with different liquids of known densities. This test is only used on loose stones that will not be affected by contact with the test liquids. An electrically *heated needle* can detect plastic imitations or plastic treatment of some gems such as turquoise.

Beyond actual identification, an appraiser takes into account the quality of the stone. The color of diamond, for example, is checked by comparing it, under strictly controlled lighting conditions, with *color comparison stones,* which are a master set of diamonds of known color grades. For other gemstones, few of which are graded with the precision of diamonds, the color quality will be judged against color chips or keys.

Unless you and your jeweler are on exceptionally good terms, you probably will have to make an appointment for an appraisal or else leave the jewelry in the shop for a few days. Be certain to get a detailed receipt for each piece you leave in the store's custody. The receipt should include a diagram showing placement of the piece's major gems.

When the appraisal has been completed, the jeweler should give you at least two copies (one for you, one for the insurance company or Internal Revenue Service) of the appraisal, which should detail in writing the following, not necessarily in this order:

1. A careful written description of the piece, ideally with an accompanying photograph, slide, or sketch.

2. Size, shape, weight, and quality of each major gemstone, and whether it is natu-

ral or synthetic. The weight of minor stones can be estimated.

3. The metal involved, and how it is worked.

4. Any damage observed on either stones or mounting.

5. An estimate of either replacement value or fair market value, or both.

6. An explanation of any grading system used in terms you can understand.

CLEANING JEWELRY

If you exercise a minimum of care and good sense when wearing your jewelry, the most you will have to do to keep most of it glowing like new will be to wipe away smudges from fingerprints with a soft cotton cloth or scrap of chamois. The cloth can be as simple as a square of old tee shirt or flannel nightgown; the chamois can be purchased from your jeweler if you do not receive one when you make your purchase.

Caution: Do not use a home ultrasonic device to clean any piece of jewelry without first discussing it with a jeweler. You could severely damage a fine gemstone by improper use of such a device, and some items must never be cleaned by this method.

A great deal of discoloration and grime can be avoided simply by acquiring the habit of putting on your jewelry at the very last, after you put on your makeup, apply perfume, and spray your hair. This is especially important with earrings and necklaces, which bear the brunt of cosmetic deposits because of their location near the face.

Removing rings and bracelets when washing your hands and while cooking, gardening, painting, doing dishes, or otherwise working near fluids or abrasives can also prevent accumulation of soap film and dirt. It is important, however, to remember where you leave your jewelry in these situations so that you can put it back on as soon as you are finished. A safe place removed from sink or washstand is preferable: at home, gems placed too near the sink can tumble down the drain; and in a public place, they can tumble into someone else's possession if you forget them.

Precious Metal

Gold and platinum unset with gemstones rarely need more than a dry wipe or a 15-minute soak in a solution of equal parts of water and mild detergent, to which you add a couple of drops of ammonia. Eliminate the ammonia for plated gold or gold of a lower alloy than 14K, because there is a chance the copper in the alloy will react with the ammonia. Polishing cloths also are available from your jeweler.

The water-detergent-ammonia bath also will remove mild tarnish from sterling and silver plate. For more serious discoloration, use a commercial silver cleaner, following the directions explicitly and taking into account the finish of your piece.

Quick dip solutions, for example, are usually fine for bright-finished and satin-finished silver, but may damage another piece by removing its decorative oxidation (blackening). Paste silver-cleaners sometimes scratch mirror finishes; a silver-cleaning cloth, available from a jeweler, is an alternative. They may work more slowly than other cleaners, but are safer for some finishes.

Precious metals set with gemstones must be cleaned very carefully to avoid damaging the gemstones. When in doubt, take the piece to a jeweler to have the job done professionally.

Gemstones

Most hard, transparent stones can be cleaned with a quick dip in alcohol to dissolve any grease that adheres from fingerprints or body oil. Diamonds need this treatment more frequently than other stones because they attract grease like a magnet. Diamond-ore processing capitalizes on this property; diamonds are separated from other stones in the mining process by running them over a grease table. The diamonds stick, while the other material flows right by.

Of the fragile gems, amber, jet, opal, tortoise shell, and turquoise should be cleaned only with a soft, dry cloth. A very thin coating of baby oil will help keep an infrequently worn opal from drying out. Pearls should be wiped with a soft, dry cloth after each wearing, and inspected periodically to see if the string (which is silk or nylon-reinforced silk in the best strands) shows signs of grime. Yearly restringing is not too often for frequently worn pearls. Coral and ivory can safely be cleaned with a damp cloth, but must be dried immediately and never exposed to commercial jewelry cleaner or any acid substance.

When in doubt, take the item to a good jewelry store and ask for advice.

SELLING YOUR JEWELRY

Having gone to all this trouble to acquire, maintain, and protect your jewelry, it may seem odd to consider selling it. In fact, there is a very major reason not to consider such a step: you'll rarely recoup even half your initial investment.

That's because the price you paid initially reflected a hefty markup over the wholesale price. Most of the time you will be lucky to recover the wholesale cost of the piece. The moral here is to select your jewelry with care, because rectifying your mistakes will probably bring you no more than petty cash.

Still, there are times when you will want to thin out your collection and dispose of seldom worn or outmoded pieces. You have several options: have the gemstones transferred to a different setting, sell by consignment through a jeweler, sell through an auction, sell to an antique dealer, or sell to a wholesaler. Options to avoid are pawn shops and attempting a private sale through a newspaper advertisement, which will only invite unwelcome visitors who may attempt to relieve you of your burden, and then some, without paying anything at all. Pawn shops usually pay less than the stingiest wholesaler.

Resetting

Most medium to large stones are worth transferring to a setting that is either more pleasing to you or more useful. Some women, for example, inherit relatives' wedding and engagement rings and have the stones remounted into cocktail rings or pins, sometimes adding colored stones. The metal in the older piece can be melted and used in the new jewelry if a custom-made piece is desired, but the money saved on the cost of the metal may very well be eclipsed by the cost of the labor involved.

A more economical alternative is to save the stones and trade in the metal for a price reduction on a ready-made setting. It is worth your time to explore both options with your jeweler. If you have your heart set on a custom-made piece but your jeweler doesn't do that sort of work, ask him or her to refer you to someone who does.

Consignment

Consignment means signing a contract with a jeweler, who will display your piece and retain a percentage of the price for which it eventually sells, usually around 15 percent. The dealer does not purchase the jewelry, but acts as a broker between you and the buyer.

Consignment contracts should specify how long the jeweler will display the item and describe the jewelry in identifiable detail in the contract. The latter is important because many items, especially rings, are very similar in appearance. You don't want to pick up someone else's less valuable diamond solitaire at the end of your consignment period.

Avoid dealers who do not insure the pieces left on consignment or who permit the jewelry to leave the store with anyone except you or the buyer.

Auction

Some larger cities have branches of the big international firms such as Christie's and Sotheby's, and almost every medium-sized community has its own auction house. Arrangements vary, but expect to pay the house 10 to 20 percent of the selling price as its commission for handling the transaction.

Antique Dealers

For jewelry of period interest—gems in Art Nouveau settings, for instance, or good Victorian era pieces—try antique dealers who specialize in jewelry. Although a dealer is likely to buy a piece outright for a fair price, expect him or her to offer it for sale at a price two to four times what you received for it. The price includes overhead and profit, plus some padding so the dealer can be "bargained down" by customers.

Take your jewelry to several dealers and compare the prices they offer; someone whose customers are primarily interested in rings and brooches, for example, might not give you as much for an amber necklace as someone whose customers are knowledgeable collectors.

Wholesalers

Coin shops and other establishments that advertise on huge yellow signs that they buy "gold, silver, class rings, etc." generally offer the lowest prices of the above options, but they are one of the few markets for old class rings, fraternal pins, and other ceremonial jewelry in the lower karats.

Shop around if there is more than one dealer convenient to you. Be very certain that you want to sell what you do sell, because chances are it will be disassembled and resold as scrap within a few days.

Glossary

(Italicized words are defined elsewhere in the glossary.)

Abalone: Shellfish with an iridescent finish that provides *mother-of-pearl*.

Achorite: Colorless *tourmaline*.

Acid Finish: A metal finish achieved by using acid to remove part of the base metal from the surface of the alloy, leaving the surface resembling the color of the more precious metal rather than the alloy.

Adelaide Ruby: Violet-red *garnet.*

Adularescence: The shimmering play of light from within a *moonstone.* Also known as *shiller.*

African Cat's Eye: Yellow and brown banded *quartz* (sometimes also used for yellow-brown *crocidolite.*) Also known as *tiger's eye.*

Agate: An opaque *quartz* that occurs in bands of varying color and transparency.

AGS: *American Gem Society.*

Alaska Diamond: *Hematite.*

Alexandrine: Synthetic *alexandrite.*

Alexandrite: A variety of *chrysoberyl* that changes from red to orange-yellow to green when viewed from different angles, appearing predominantly green in daylight and red or purplish in incandescent light.

Alloy: A mixture of metals that uses desirable properties of each to achieve specific effects, usually added strength and specific color.

Almandine: Purple *garnet.*

Almandine Spinel: Violet *spinel.*

Aluminum: A metallic element used as a precious metal from 1855 until it became widely available in the late 1880s.

Amazonite: A variety of green *feldspar.*

+ **Amber:** Fossilized tree resin.

+ **American Gem Society:** Trade association of fine jewelers.

+ **Amethyst:** Transparent, violet *quartz*.

+ **Apache Tear:** Polished *obsidian*.

+ **Apple Jade:** *Chrysoprase*.

+ **Appliqué:** Pieces of metal soldered onto other metal.

+ **Appraisal:** An expert's valuation of a piece of jewelry.

+ **Aquamarine:** Pale blue-green *beryl*.

+ **Aqua Regia:** Mix of concentrated nitric and hydrochloric acids, one of the very few substances that can dissolve gold.

+ **Arizona Ruby:** *Garnet*.

+ **Assay:** To test a metal to determine its quality.

+ **Asterism:** A star-like phenomenon found in several gemstones, especially rubies and sapphires, caused by the presence of *rutile*. The "star" can have either four or six points, or, in less valuable stones, be a mere fuzzy line.

+ **Australian Ruby:** *Garnet*.

+ **Aventurine (also spelled "avanturine"):** *Sunstone* or *quartz*.

+ **Avoirdupois Weight:** System of weights used in the United States, based on the grain, dram, ounce, and pound.

Azurite: Bright-blue copper carbonate.

Baguette: Small gemstone, usually cut in a narrow rectangle, used in designs to give contrast to larger stones.

Balas Ruby: *Spinel.*

Bangle: A rigid bracelet or anklet, often with no clasp.

Baroque Pearl: A *pearl* of irregular shape.

Basse-taille: An enameling technique in which metal is engraved or carved in low relief and then covered with translucent *enamel.*

Beryl: A silicon-based mineral, the finest specimens of which are *emerald* and *aquamarine.*

Bezel: A round collar into which a gemstone is set.

Biwa Pearl: A freshwater *pearl* from Lake Biwa, Japan, cultured by using a bit of oyster flesh rather than a *mother-of-pearl* core.

Black Finish: An *oxide finish* on metal.

Black Opal: An *opal,* colored peacock blue to slate gray, with lots of fire.

Blister Pearl: A half *pearl* formed against a mollusk's shell.

Bloodstone: Dark green opaque *quartz* with nodules of bright red *jasper.*

Bog Oak: Jewelry carved from oak that has been preserved in peat bogs.

- **Bohemian Garnet:** Wine-red *garnet*.

- **Bone Amber:** White *amber*.

- **Bone Ivory:** Jewelry carved from bone.

- **Borax:** Cheap, shoddy merchandise, so called because the mineral borax is used to produce glass.

- **Bouillon:** Clear soup made from chicken, beef, or fish stock. See *bullion*.

- **Bowenite:** *Serpentine,* often used as a *jade* substitute.

- **Brazil Emerald:** Green *tourmaline*.

- **Brazil Ruby:** Pink *topaz*.

- **Bright Cut:** Sharp-edged engraving that sparkles.

- **Bright Polished:** Metal polished to a mirror-like finish. Compare *plain polished*.

- **Brilliant Cut:** A round, 58-faceted gemstone cut that shows a maximum of the stone's fire and brilliance.

- **Briolette:** A gemstone cut in an elongated teardrop with bands of triangular or rectangular facets.

- **Britannia Standard:** *Silver* that is 958 parts pure, as compared with *sterling,* which is 925 parts pure.

- **Brooch:** An ornamental pin.

- **Brush Finish:** A soft dull metal finish produced by a *scratch brush*.

- **Bullion:** 24K gold formed into bars, ingots, or plate.

Burnish: To polish metal by rubbing it with a smooth, hard tool such as a polishing stone.

Cabochon: The convex surface of a gemstone.

Cairngorm: Yellow or smoky brown clear *quartz* from the Cairngorm mountains of Scotland.

Californite: *Vesuvianite,* a jade substitute.

Cameo: Raised relief carving on a gemstone or shell.

Cape Ruby: *Garnet.*

Carat: A measure of gemstone weight equivalent to .200 gram. In the United States, "carat" is exclusive to weight, but in some other English-speaking countries it is also a measure of the purity of precious metals.

Carnelian: Translucent semiprecious *quartz.*

Cast: To form an object by pouring melted metal into a mold.

Cat's Eye: A gem that exhibits *chatoyancy.*

Cave Onyx: Marble. See *Mexican onyx.*

Ceylon Diamond: Colorless *zircon.*

Chalcedony: Translucent to opaque *quartz* that is fine grained and has a waxy luster when polished. Also called *cryptocrystalline quartz.*

Champlevé: An enameling technique in which depressions engraved in metal are filled with *enamel.*

Chase: To define the form of a metalwork design by hammering from the front of the piece to raise, depress, or push aside the metal.

Chatoyancy: An optical phenomenon that results in a luminous band appearing on the surface of a *cabochon*-cut gemstone.

Chrysoberyl: A hard gem species that includes *alexandrite* and the most valuable form of *cat's eye*.

Chrysoprase: Apple-green *chalcedony*.

Citrine: Transparent yellow to brownish *quartz*.

Cleavage: The tendency of a *crystal* to break along the planes of its crystal form.

Cloisonné: Enameling technique in which metal strips or wire are soldered onto other metal and the resulting spaces filled with *enamel*.

Coin Silver: *Silver* that once was silver money.

Concha: Oval silver pieces strung together with leather to form a belt.

Coral: Exterior remains of colonies of sea creatures used as gemstones when the colors are pleasing.

Corundum: Rare, very hard *mineral* that includes rubies and sapphires.

Corundum Cat's Eye: An imperfect *star sapphire*.

Costume Jewelry: Jewelry, usually inexpensive, made from non-precious materials.

Crocidolite: Gray-blue to grass-green *mineral* that exhibits *chatoyancy* under certain natural chemical changes. See *tiger's eye, hawk's eye.*

Crown: In gemstone terminology, the upper portion of a faceted stone.

Cryptocrystalline Quartz: *Quartz* that occurs in fine-grained translucent or opaque masses, such as *agate.*

Crystal: Geometric pattern formed by molecules of a mineral.

Crystal Lattice: The repetition of crystals that forms a structure specific to each gemstone species.

Crystalline Quartz: *Quartz* that occurs in large, transparent masses, such as *amethyst* or *rock crystal.*

Cubic Zirconia: Synthetic *zircon* used as a diamond substitute.

Culet: The small, flat *facet* at the bottom of a *brilliant-cut* gemstone.

Cultured Pearl: A *pearl* artificially seeded, either with a small *mother-of-pearl* bead or a bit of oyster flesh.

Cymophane: *Chrysoberyl,* especially *cat's eye.*

Damascene: Either a moire-like pattern on metal or metal decorated with inlays of silver, gold, or a combination of the two.

De Beers: The marketing organization for most of the diamonds produced by the free world.

Demantoid: Green *garnet,* one of the gemstone's most valuable forms. Sometimes called *olivine.*

Diamond: The hardest naturally-occurring substance known, a gemstone in its transparent form, naturally occurring in many colors.

Dichroic: Having color that changes as the gem is turned.

Die Stamp: To strike metal with heavy blows from a drop hammer that compress the atoms, thus strengthening the metal. If the hammer and anvil are dies, a design can be stamped as well.

Dispersion: The separation of light into its component colors, as through a prism.

Doublet: The fusion of two layers of material to create the appearance of a single gemstone. A true doublet is composed of two gemstones of equivalent value; a false doublet is a gemstone backed by a larger piece of less valuable material.

Dravite: Brown *tourmaline.*

Draw Plate: A flat piece of steel pierced with holes of graduated size, used to change the shape or reduce the size of a wire.

Drop Cut: A gemstone cut into an elongated pear or teardrop shape. See *briolette.*

Ductility: The ease with which a metal can be drawn into wire.

Durability: A gemstone's resistance to scratching.

Electroplating: Plating a metal by means of an electrical charge.

Emboss: To ornament metal in raised relief, usually by pushing aside rather than removing the metal.

Emerald: Bright green *beryl*.

Emerald Cut: An oblong gemstone cut having 58 facets.

Enamel: Powdered glass fused to metal through heat.

En Cabochon: *Cabochon* cut.

English Finish: A highly polished plating of 24K gold on an alloy.

Engrave: To ornament metal by cutting it away with small chisels, called gravers.

En Résille: A design cut into *rock crystal* or *paste,* lined with gold and then opaque or transparent enamel. It resembles *cloisonné.*

Estate Jewelry: Second-hand jewelry.

Etch: To decorate the surface of a metal by dissolving a portion of it with acid.

Evening Emerald: *Peridot.*

Facet: A flat, polished surface on a cut gemstone, usually having three or four sides.

Fashion Jewelry: Costume jewelry.

- **Faux:** False.

- **Feldspar:** A mineral species that includes *moonstone* and *sunstone*.

- **Filigree:** A delicate, lacelike ornament made from gold or silver wire.

- **Finding:** Mounting for jewelry.

- **Fire:** The flash of light from the interior of a gemstone.

- **Fire Opal:** Orange, red, or yellow *opal* with lots of fire.

- **Fluorescence:** The glow of certain gemstones under ultraviolet light.

- **Fool's Gold:** *Pyrite.*

- **Forge:** In the metalwork sense, to shape heated metal on an anvil with a hammer. The process compresses the metal, strengthening it.

- **Fossil Ivory:** Jewelry carved from the tusks of the extinct woolly mammoth.

- **Freshwater Pearl:** A *pearl* formed in a freshwater shellfish rather than an oyster.

- **Frosted Finish:** *Sandblast* finish.

- **Full Cut:** Gemstone with 57 facets, one less than a *brilliant cut.*

- **Fun Pearl:** Imitation *pearl.*

- **Gadroon:** Curved pieces set vertically or slightly spiraled.

165

Garnet: A gemstone usually thought of as wine-red in color, although it occurs in a rainbow of tints. See *almandine, demantoid, grossularite, pyrope, topazolite.*

Gem: A gemstone cut and polished for setting in a piece of jewelry.

Gemological Institute of America: The jewelry industry's education, research, and testing arm.

Gemstone: A mineral or other substance that can be cut and polished for ornament.

German Silver: *Nickel silver.*

GIA: *Gemological Institute of America.*

Gild: To decorate the surface of a metal or gemstone with gold or a design in gold.

Girdle: The widest part of a faceted stone.

Gold: A yellow metal that is easily worked, does not tarnish, and is virtually indestructible.

Gold Electroplate: Gold coating accomplished through *electroplating.*

Gold Filled: Base metal coated with an outer layer of gold alloy that accounts for more than 1/20th of its weight.

Gold Flashed: Extremely thin gold electroplate.

Gold Overlay: *Gold plate.*

Gold Plate: A deposit of gold that covers base metal or silver.

Goldtone: Gold-colored metal that does not contain gold.

Gold Washed: *Gold flashed.*

Gooseberry Garnet: *Grossularite.*

Granulation: Tiny gold balls used to decorate metal.

Green Gold: 18K gold alloyed with silver, or 14K and 10K gold alloyed with silver, zinc, and copper. It has a greenish cast.

Grisaille: *Enamel* in black, white, and shades of gray.

Grossularite: Transparent to translucent *garnet* sometimes sold as a jade substitute. Also known as *gooseberry garnet.*

Gutta-percha: A compound of latex, resin, and sawdust used in 19th-century costume jewelry.

Hair Jewelry: Jewelry either made from, or made to enclose a lock of, human hair.

Hammered Finish: Metal finish produced by hammering tiny overlapping dents on the surface.

Handcrafted: Made entirely by hand tools.

Hand Finished: Code for machine-made jewelry with a minimum of hand work.

Handwrought: Handcrafted.

Harlequin Opal: *Opal* from Czechoslovakia having lots of fire.

Hawk's Eye: Gray-blue or green *crocidolite*.

Heliodor: Yellow *beryl*.

Heliotrope: *Bloodstone*.

Hematite: Black, opaque form of iron oxide, easily carved.

Herkimer Diamond: *Rock crystal* found in Herkimer County of New York state.

Hessonite: *Grossularite*.

Hiddenite: Green *spodumene*.

Idocrase: *Vesuvianite*.

Imperial Jade: The finest *jadeite*.

India Finish: Olive smudge in the background of *green gold alloy*, with raised surfaces polished to produce a contrast.

Indian Arts and Crafts Association (IACA): A trade group formed to encourage ethical behavior by dealers in Native American jewelry.

Indian Jewelry: Most commonly, silver jewelry produced by four Native American tribes in the southwestern United States.

Indicolite: Blue *tourmaline*.

Inlay: One metal or gemstone set into the surface of another.

Intaglio: A design carved below the surface of a gemstone or a metal. The opposite of *cameo*.

Iridium: One of the *platinum* metals.

Ivory: Elephant tusk, walrus tusk, bone, or the nut of certain palm trees. Elephant ivory is the most valuable.

Jacinth: Orange *zircon*.

Jade: *Jadeite* or *nephrite,* classically green but available in a variety of other colors as well.

Jadeite: The harder of the *jade* minerals, chemically a silicate of sodium and aluminum. First discovered in the New World.

Japan Pearl: A cultured *blister pearl.*

Jasper: Opaque, non-translucent *quartz* of a dark brownish red.

Jet: Fossil coal.

Jewel: A gemstone set in precious metal.

Jewelry: Objects used for personal adornment.

Jewelry Floater: An insurance policy for fine jewelry.

Karat: Term used to define the fineness of gold in the United States (some other countries use the "karat" spelling for gemstone weight as well as gold). Pure gold is 24K. 18K is 75% gold, 25% alloy.

Kunzite: Pink to rose-colored *spodumene.*

Lacquer: Unfused *enamel* used on larger pieces of jewelry or objects that are fairly well protected from scratching and chipping. Lacquer is softer than fused, or heat-bonded, enamel.

Lapis Lazuli: Deep blue opaque mineral, sometimes flecked with gold or *pyrite* (fool's gold).

Lavaliere: An ornament hung from a chain worn around the neck, usually a small jeweled gold *locket.*

Locket: A small, flat hinged case for pictures or locks of hair, usually worn suspended from a chain or *brooch.*

Lost Wax: A casting process in which a wax model encased in a sand mold is melted away before hot metal is poured into the mold.

Malachite: An opaque copper mineral of light and dark bands of green.

Malleability: The ease with which a metal can be worked.

Marcasite: A mineral with a bronze luster. Also a name for *pyrite,* a more durable mineral.

Marquise Cut: A gemstone cut of 58 facets in the shape of a pointed oval.

Matara Diamond: Colorless *zircon.*

Matt(e) Finish: *Brush finish.*

Melee: Small stones used to enhance larger ones.

Metal: An opaque substance that shows a characteristic luster, conducts electricity and heat, can be fused, shaped, and drawn into wire.

+ **Mexican Jade:** Green-dyed marble.

+ **Mexican Onyx:** Banded, mottled marble that is easily carved into curios.

+ **Mikimoto Pearl:** Trademarked name for a cultured *pearl*.

+ **Mineral:** Inorganic solids formed by natural processes, usually crystalline in structure.

+ **Mohs Scale:** A measure of a gemstone's resistance to scratching (hardness).

+ **Mollusk:** Shellfish, especially oysters and mussels, that produce pearls.

+ **Momme:** Unit of weight for cultured pearls.

+ **Moonstone:** A grayish, watery form of *feldspar* that has a shimmering white or blue sheen.

+ **Morganite:** Pink *beryl*.

+ **Moss Agate:** Light-colored *agate* shot through with tiny, dark patterns, often greenish, that resemble moss.

+ **Mother-of-Pearl:** The iridescent lining of a *mollusk* shell.

+ **Mother of Ruby:** *Spinel.*

+ **Nacre:** Iridescent material secreted by pearl-producing *mollusks.*

+ **Natural Pearl:** A *pearl* formed without human help.

Navette: *Marquise cut* stone or boat-shaped setting.

Necklace: A string of beads or other small objects worn about the neck. Literally, "lace for the neck."

Nephrite: The *jade* of the Orient. A compound of calcium and magnesium, nephrite is the softer of the two jade minerals but is tougher than *jadeite*.

New Jade: *Serpentine.*

Nickel Silver: An alloy of copper, zinc, and nickel used for imitation silver jewelry and inexpensive flatware.

Niello: An engraved design filled with a blue-black alloy.

Obsidian: A natural volcanic glass, black or gray in color.

Occidental Cat's Eye: Greenish *quartz.*

Olivine: *Peridot,* although sometimes used to refer to *demantoid garnet.*

Onyx: Black- and white-banded *chalcedony.*

Opal: Iridescent, translucent *quartz* in a form that resembles a hardened gel.

Oregon Jade: Green *jasper.*

Orient: The characteristic glow and interplay of colors on the surface of a good *pearl.*

Oriental Amethyst: Purple *corundum.*

Oriental Cat's Eye: *Chrysoberyl.*

Oriental Moonstone: Precious *moonstone.*

Oriental Ruby: Genuine *ruby.*

Oriental Topaz: Yellow *sapphire.*

Osmium: A *platinum* metal, usually alloyed with other platinums for strength and hardness. Used to tip gold pen-points for wear resistance.

Oxide Finish: Black finish on metals, usually a background for raised, polished designs.

Paillons: Tiny figures stamped from very thin sheets of gold, used to decorate *enamel.*

Palladium: One of the *platinum* metals; when alloyed with gold, yields *white gold* of the highest quality.

Parure: A matched set of jewelry, such as earrings, necklace, bracelet, brooch, and ring.

Paste: Fine glass that simulates the look of fine gemstones.

Patina: The condition of a metal surface after years of exposure to the atmosphere and wear.

Pavé Set: Small gemstones set side by side, hiding the underlying metal.

Pavilion: The base of a faceted gemstone.

Pawn Silver: Native American tribal jewelry purchased in a pawn shop.

Pearl: A gemstone formed inside a shellfish.

Pendant: An ornament suspended from a neckchain, necklace, or earring.

Peridot: A variety of *olivine,* distinctive for its luster and color, which can range from grass green to a deep bottle green.

Pink Gold: Gold alloyed with silver and less copper than *red gold.*

Plain Polished: Metal polished without further ornamentation.

Platinum: Heavy non-tarnishing silver-white precious metal. There are six metals in the platinum family.

Plique-à-jour: Enamel suspended between metal strips in the manner of stained glass.

Point: One one-hundredth of a *carat.*

Prase: Grass green *chalcedony.*

Precious Cat's Eye: *Chrysoberyl.*

Pressed Amber: *Amber* that has been melted down and reheated to form a solid.

Prism Spectroscope: Instrument for measuring a gemstone's absorption of light.

Pyrite: Opaque, brassy metal composed of iron sulfide, sometimes sold as *marcasite,* although the latter is less durable. Also known as *fool's gold.*

Pyrolusite: Crystallized form of manganese that forms the "moss" in *moss agate.*

Pyrope: Deep red *garnet.*

Quartz: A silicon dioxide found in nearly every mineral on the face of the earth. It occurs in two groups: large, clear transparent pieces such as rock crystal, and translucent or opaque masses such as agate and jasper.

Red Gold: A gold alloy with a high copper content.

Refractive Index: The specific angle at which a particular gemstone species bends light.

Refractometer: An instrument for measuring the angle at which a gemstone bends light.

Relief: Design raised or lowered from the surface of the metal or gemstone.

Repoussé: A raised design hammered into metal from the back of the piece.

Rhinestone: Originally, *rock crystal* from the Rhine Valley of Germany, now also a faceted sparkling glass "gemstone."

Rhodium: One of the *platinum* metals. Used mainly for plating other metals.

Rock Crystal: Transparent colorless *quartz.*

Rolled Gold: Gold plate formed by applying one or several sheets of gold to a base metal under heat or pressure.

Roman Finish: Electroplated 24K gold dulled by a *scratch brush.*

Rondelle: A bead used as a spacer between two more valuable or more decorative beads.

Rose Cut: A gemstone cut with a flat base, a circular or oval top with up to 32 triangular facets, and a domed point, so named because it resembles a rosebud about to open.

Rose Finish: A background smudge of *pink gold* that contrasts with the yellow gold in the foreground design.

Rose Gold: *Pink gold.*

Rose Quartz: Pink *quartz,* sometimes cloudy with *rutile* inclusions.

Rough: Gemstone material not yet cut and polished.

Rubellite: Pink *tourmaline.*

Ruby: Transparent red *corundum.*

Ruby Spinel: Red *spinel.*

Ruthenium: Hard, white *platinum* metal used mainly as a hardener.

Rutile: Needle-like crystals often completely surrounded by other minerals. If lined up in certain ways, produce *asterism.*

Sandblast Finish: Frosted metal finish produced by a highly pressurized stream of sand.

Sapphire: Blue *corundum,* although other colors of corundum except red also are sold as sapphire.

Sard: Light to dark brown *chalcedony,* distinguished from *jasper* by its translucency.

Sardonyx: Bands of *sard* and white *chalcedony.*

Satin Finish: Soft, pearly finish for metal.

Schorl: Black *tourmaline.*

Scratch Brush: A brush of hardened metal used to impart a dull finish on a metal surface.

Scrimshaw: Decorative carving on whalebone or other bone, or ivory. Genuine whalebone is the most valuable.

Seed Pearl: Tiny round *pearl,* usually used in masses or rows.

Serpentine: A mineral used mainly as an inexpensive substitute for *jade.*

Sheffield Plate: One of the earliest methods of silver plating, developed in Sheffield, England.

Shell Cameo: *Cameo* carved from a seashell.

Shiller: The shimmering play of light from the interior of a *moonstone.* Also known as *adularescence.*

Siberian Ruby: Red *tourmaline.*

Silk: In the gemstone sense, the soft, whitish sheen to *corundum,* especially *sapphire,* caused by minute inclusions of *rutile.*

Silver: A comparatively scarce, brilliant white metal, easily worked.

Simulated Pearl: Imitation *pearl.*

Single Cut: Gemstone with 17 facets.

Smoky Quartz: Light brown to nearly black transparent *quartz.*

Smoky Topaz: Usually *citrine* or *smoky quartz.*

Specific Gravity: The weight of a gem compared to the weight of an equal volume of water.

Spinel: A mineral that resembles *ruby* in its red and pink forms.

Spodumene: A transparent mineral most valued in its light green form *(hiddenite)* or pink and rose form *(kunzite).*

Squash Blossom Necklace: A Native American tribal necklace consisting of hollow beads and flower forms, with a crescent *pendant.*

Stabilized Turquoise: Good-quality *turquoise* that has been impregnated with plastic to ensure color permanence.

Step Cut: A gemstone cut with rows of long, narrow four-sided facets parallel to the *girdle.*

Sterling: A silver alloy of 925 parts pure silver and 75 parts copper.

Stomacher: An ornament worn at the front of the upper body.

Sunstone: Reddish variety of *feldspar* with minute inclusions of iron oxide that sparkle.

Swedge: A relief technique that decorates metal by forcing it into the grooves of an iron block.

Swiss Cut: A gemstone with 33 facets.

Table: The large center facet in the crown of a *gemstone*.

Taille d'Épergne: Engraving filled with *enamel*, usually blue or black. This technique is the reverse of *champlevé*.

Tarnish: Discoloration of metal caused by exposure to the atmosphere.

Tenacity: A measure of how well a gemstone resists breaking.

Tiger's Eye: Yellow-brown *crocidolite*, or sometimes, yellow- and brown-banded quartz.

Topaz: Valuable silicate gemstone with brilliant fire, most prized when the color of fine dry sherry.

Topazolite: Yellowish *garnet*.

Topaz Quartz: *Citrine*.

Tortoise Shell: The shell of the hawksbill turtle, translucent golden yellow with brown markings.

Tourmaline: A transparent gemstone, relatively tough and hard, that comes in a wide variety of colors, including some crystals that may display two or three colors at once.

Treated Turquoise: Low-quality *turquoise* that has been dyed to enhance color and treated with plastic to prevent fracture.

Triplet: A fusion of three layers of material to create what appears to be one gemstone, usually with the more valuable stone sandwiched between two of lesser value. Compare *doublet.*

Troy Weight: System used by pharmacists and jewelers, based on 12 ounces to a pound, with an ounce equivalent to 480 grains or 20 pennyweights.

Turquoise: Blue to greenish opaque gemstone, most frequently associated with Native American tribal designs.

Uralian Emerald: Green *garnet.*

Vegetable Ivory: Jewelry carved from the whitish nuts of certain palm trees.

Vermeil: Gold-plated silver, bronze, or copper.

Vesuvianite: Common silicate mineral, the green variety of which is *californite,* often substituted for *jade.*

Watch Fob: A short ribbon or chain that attaches a pocket watch to a pocket. Can also refer to ornaments at the end of such a chain or ribbon.

Water Opal: Bluish, white, pink, or greenish *opal* with good color play.

White Gold: Alloy of *gold* with copper, zinc and nickel, or gold with *palladium,* so that the resulting metal resembles *silver* or *platinum.*

✦ **White Metal:** Alloy of 90% tin, 9% antimony, 1% copper, used for imitation silver jewelry.

✦ **Yellow Gold:** The classic alloy of gold with copper and silver, the alloy that most closely resembles the metal's natural color.

✦ **Zircon:** A fiery transparent gemstone that's softer and more abundant than *diamond*.

Appendix

Table 1   Taking the Measure of Precious Metals

Troy weight is an ancient system of measurement that survives today in the precious metals and pharmaceutical industries. It differs significantly from the avoirdupois system commonly used in the United States today; someday, like the avoirdupois system, it may be replaced by the metric system.

---

1 troy ounce = 480 grains

= 20 pennyweights

= 1.097 avoirdupois ounces

= 31.103 grams

1 troy pound = 12 troy ounces

= 5760 grains

= 240 pennyweights

= 13.164 avoirdupois ounces

= 0.82275 avoirdupois pounds

= 373.236 grams

Table 2 Hardness and Durability

Mohs Scale of Hardness*	Stone
10	Diamond
9	Corundum (ruby, sapphire)
8½	Chrysoberyl
8	Spinel, topaz
8 to 7½	Beryl (emerald, aquamarine)
7½ to 7	Garnet, tourmaline
7½ to 6½	Zircon
7	Quartz
7 to 6½	Chalcedony, peridot, jadeite
6½ to 6	Nephrite
6½ to 5	Opal
6	Moonstone
6 to 5	Glass, lapis, turquoise
5½ to 5	Obsidian, serpentine
4½ to 4	Platinum
4½ to 2½	Pearl
4	Fluorite
4 to 2½	Jet
3½	Coral, conch, pearl
3	Black coral
3 to 2½	Copper
3 to 2	Ivory
2½	Silver
2½ to 2	Amber, gold
2	Alabaster, gypsum
1	Talc

*Numbers reflect only the order of hardness, not the degree.

Table 3   Gemstone Durability*

Faceted Stones	Stones Generally Shaped en Cabochon
Corundum (ruby, sapphire)	Nephrite
Diamond	Jadeite
Spinel	Chalcedony
Chrysoberyl	Hematite
Quartz	Lapis
Garnet	Coral
Tourmaline	Pearl
Synthetic emerald	Shell
Beryl	Turquoise
Topaz	Amber
Peridot	Opal

*Listed in descending order of durability (toughness, tenacity, resistance to fracture) within each category. A stone in nontraditional shape (e.g., a faceted bead of lapis) may be more or less durable than a comparable stone cut en cabochon.)

Table 4 Birthstones

The following are the traditional natural stones associated with the various months in the United States, Canada, Great Britain, Australia, and South Africa. Where alternatives are given, the second choice is usually a less expensive substitute for the first.

January	Garnet. *Alternate:* tourmaline (South Africa).
February	Amethyst.
March	Aquamarine. *Alternate:* bloodstone (United States, Great Britain, Australia).
April	Diamond. *Alternates:* rock crystal (Great Britain), zircon (Australia), colorless sapphire (South Africa).
May	Emerald. *Alternates:* chrysoprase (Great Britain), green tourmaline (Australia).
June	Pearl; cameo (Australia). *Alternates:* moonstone (United States, Great Britain, Australia), alexandrite (United States).
July	Ruby. *Alternate:* carnelian (Great Britain, Australia).
August	Peridot. *Alternates:* sardonyx (United States, Great Britain, Australia, Canada); green tourmaline (South Africa).
September	Sapphire. *Alternates:* lapis lazuli (Great Britain, Australia.)
October	Opal. *Alternates:* pink tourmaline (United States), tiger's eye (Canada).
November	Topaz. *Alternate:* citrine (United States).
December	Turquoise; onyx (Canada only). *Alternate:* zircon (United States, Canada).

Index

INDEX

Anne Bingham is a journalist and collector of antique jewelry. She lives in Milwaukee, Wisconsin.